BECAUSE YOU'RE MINE

A GUNVOR STRÖM NOVEL

LUNA MILLER

This book is a work of fiction. The characters and events in this book are fictitious. Any similarity to any persons, living or dead, is confidential and not intended by the Author.

Copyright © 2021 by Luna Miller

All rights reserved, including the right to reproduce this book or portions thereof in any form whatsoever.

For information, address Publish Authority, 300 Colonial Center Parkway, Suite 100, Roswell, GA 30076.

Cover design lead: Raeghan Rebstock
Translator: Ludvig Christensen Parment
Editor: Nancy Laning

Publish Authority offices in
Roswell (Atlanta), GA and Newport Beach, CA USA

The Library of Congress has established a Cataloging-in-Publication record for this title.

ISBN: 978-1-954000-03-2

PublishAuthority.com

PRAISE FOR "LOOKING FOR ALICE"—
BOOK #1 IN THE GUNVOR STRÖM
SERIES:

In Gunvor Ström, Miller...has crafted an entertaining heroine – a modern Miss Marple with a social conscience and some impressive aikido skills. ...a highly enjoyable read.
    A....punchy Nordic Noir thriller.

—*KIRKUS REWIEWS*

Translated by Ludvig Christensen Parment

So many books, so little time.

                    FRANK ZAPPA

PREFACE

Gunvor Ström is a former surgeon, maybe in her sixties. Her hands might be too shaky to perform operations, but her mind is sharp as a scalpel. Instead of retiring, which she totally refuses to do, she joins a Stockholm detective agency.

In one of her previous cases—*Looking for Alice*—Gunvor runs into problems to perform her work. She does not fit in at Stockholm´s hot nightspots, where she must spy on a man who is suspected of infidelity. So, she finds herself two unlikely allies who fit in perfectly. David is a young, jobless waster who hangs about Fruängen Tube station. And, 19-year-old Elin is shy and introverted after spending too long in her bedroom hiding from her parents´ constant fighting.

The plan is that they shall be Gunvor´s eyes and ears in the hectic nightlife. It works. They do what they are told. But only to a certain extent. Eager to make a difference, they take big risks. And suddenly, it is clear that this case is much worse than one of infidelity. A murder is committed, and more lives, including theirs, are threatened.

PREFACE

Against all odds, they escape their brush with death and manage to solve the case. Barely.

Still, they all want more. So, when a husband is reported missing...

Welcome to the second book in the Gunvor Ström series.

CHAPTER 1
THURSDAY, OCTOBER 29

HE COULDN'T HELP CRACKING up in a big stupid grin, even though he was aware that he must have looked absolutely ridiculous to the people passing by on the street. Why should he care? He hadn't felt this alive in years. What harm was there in letting people see how happy he was?

It was early morning. The air was cold, but he enjoyed it. A new day and, hopefully, a new beginning. People he met were rushing to work with sober minds. Everybody seemed in a hurry. Not him. If he could, he would have stopped the world for a while just before they had to separate. Just before, the train had left with his new acquaintance. His new love.

They had just had one night together. But he was sure this was it. Even if it was a long time since he last felt this way, he knew that he was falling in love. They just had to meet again. And they would. Already next weekend.

He was so engrossed in his thoughts and fantasies that he did not notice that the gate never closed behind him as he entered the apartment building. He did not hear the quiet footsteps, swiftly bounding up the staircase as he got into the beautiful, old elevator and slowly ascended to the third floor. He neither heard nor saw anything out of the ordinary as he fiddled with the keys and finally managed to unlock the door to his apartment.

It was not until he stepped into the bright hallway and a quiet shadow pushed through the door behind him that he became aware that everything was wrong.

CHAPTER 2
THE DAY BEFORE - WEDNESDAY, OCTOBER 28

AIDAN HAD JUST ORDERED his second glass of red wine when Drew came back from the dance floor, greedily gulping down the last sips of his beer. He had a big smile on his face, and his forehead glistered from beads of sweat. They had both had their fair share to drink that night, and Aidan was getting a little tired, but he could see that Drew was in very high spirits. And at that moment, that was all that mattered. Earlier that afternoon, Aidan had picked up Drew by the flight buses at the Stockholm city terminal. They had taken the subway to Östermalmstorg together and walked the short distance to Tudor Arms on Grevgatan. Being true Englishmen, they appreciated the genuine pub atmosphere and the bartender's banter as they were each served a pint of pale ale.

They had managed to find a quiet corner in the establishment, where they could talk freely and undisturbed. Drew had been dumped again, and it was Aidan's job to console him. His boyfriend had turned out to be a real pig. It was not like Drew had expected anything else but being left in favor of "some pathetic B-list celebrity," as he described it, had hit a sore spot.

He had never been much for long-lasting relationships anyway. It had been a matter of wounded pride rather than a broken heart. Fortunately, the healing process was quick. After a vegetarian garden burger and a couple of Kilkennys, all had been forgiven, if not forgotten, and Drew was back in his usual good mood.

When Drew had phoned Aidan a few days earlier to ask if he could come down from London for a heart to heart, Aidan had already anticipated a long night and made sure to cancel any early appointments for the next day. Drew had a light-hearted and carefree personality by nature and was not one to hold onto grudges and failures. It was very rare for him to come across a hardship that couldn't be cured by a good party or a night on the town. So, when the waiter had taken their empty plates and Drew was chatting away over their third beer, Aidan tried to remind himself as to which of Stockholm's gay clubs he liked the most. Less than an hour later, he found himself in the lounge at Club Nype, watching Drew let it rip on the house dancefloor.

Even though it made Aidan happy to see his friend shine once again, he was aware that, for himself, the boring part of the night had just begun. He had always been self-conscious about dancing, and it did not seem likely that he would find anyone who would be up for spending the evening making conversation with him. Most people probably did not visit Club Nype to find another straight friend, he thought. And it would be wrong to raise any false expectations. Not that he thought of himself as very attractive. But still. So, he prepared himself to spend the rest of the night sitting by himself, trying to look busy and not too alone and pathetic.

After finishing his beer, rather than taking a seat next to Aidan, Drew sauntered off to the bar and, after a little while, reappeared with two new beers. He was already too drunk to remember that Aidan had switched over to wine. It didn't matter. Aidan smiled approvingly and nodded when Drew greedily drank half of his beer in one go and asked if it was okay for him to return to the dancefloor.

After spending countless nights out with Drew in Stockholm, London and Manchester, Aidan rated this club among the better ones. But he did miss the company and conversations with his friend from earlier in the evening. Drew was an old and dear friend, but they didn't have the opportunity to see each other as often as Aiden would like. They had a lot to talk about when they did, but right now, Drew was preoccupied.

Suddenly, something in the bar caught Aidan's attention. A woman, roughly his own age, lashed out at one of the bartenders. She held her phone and waved it in the air like she was eager to show him something on it. The bartender didn't show any sign of interest and made a dismissive gesture with his free hand and rolled his eyes as he walked past her, carrying a tray full of drinks. Aidan looked at the woman. The intensity she had displayed during the conversation with the bartender soon faded, and she just stood there. He thought the woman looked lost and vulnerable. Her eyes swept over the crowd as if she was looking for someone, and at one point, their eyes met. Aidan waved at her. At first, she looked all around her to see if the wave was meant for someone else, but when she realized that it wasn't, she took a few hesitant steps towards him with a surprised look on her face.

"Hi there, are you okay? Can I help you with anything?" Aidan tried his best to appear as sober as possible. He was both eager to have someone to talk to and genuinely curious about what she was doing.

"Well," she hesitated. "I'm not sure. Maybe." He saw a

glimmer of hope in her pretty eyes. "Do you know this person?" She held up a picture on her phone.

Aidan took his time inspecting it thoroughly even though he could tell right away that he did not recognize the man in the photo. It was a well-groomed man in an expensive-looking suit. He looked neat and stylish. It must have been a professional portrait photo, probably taken for use at work or some official presentation. Aidan thought that the man, much like himself, did not seem to fit in at Club Nype. The patrons of the club were a hipper and more extreme. But then again, he may well have another side to him once the workday is over and the tie and jacket come off.

"Sorry, I haven't seen him. I'm not exactly a regular here. I just came with a gay friend tonight." Aidan made sure to point out to the woman with the beautiful eyes that he wasn't gay himself. "Should he be here?"

"I don't know. He's been missing. I don't know, I just thought maybe..."

"Oh, I'm sorry to hear that. You know what? I have some experience with missing persons investigations and that sort of thing. I would be happy to help if I can."

"Some" is a relative term, he thought to himself. His friend, Gunvor, a private investigator by profession, would probably have accused him of lying. With some merit, admittedly. But at the same time, he felt sure that he knew more about the subject than most people, given all the late nights of bouncing ideas and theories back and forth with Gunvor for her cases. Surely Gunvor would understand that he didn't want to let an opportunity like this escape him. Sitting bored and abandoned in a gay club, and suddenly a pretty woman turns up, in need of someone—for him—to help save the day.

"May I have a seat?"

Suddenly her voice sounded almost pitiful.

"Of course, I'm sorry! Where are my manners?"

Like many of his countrymen, Aidan took pride in his politeness. He felt ashamed and immediately stood up and pulled out the chair next to his. Not that it would have been necessary, but he wanted to compensate for having kept her standing, and he could tell she appreciated the gesture.

"So, what happened?"

"It's one of my best friends. His name is Seb. He has just —vanished."

"Oh, eerie. How long has he been missing? Have you talked to anyone in his family?"

Aidan had to restrain himself from asking too many questions at the same time. The woman lingered with her answer. She was sitting very still, with her eyes fixed on the sticky tabletop. Aidan was not sure whether she had heard him and wondered to himself whether he should repeat the question. But just then, she lifted her gaze and looked at Aidan with tear-filled eyes.

"I haven't heard from him in about a week. We usually talk almost every day." She wiped away a single tear that was making its way down her cheek before she continued. "All I know is that he was off to see someone. But I don't know who. He sees a lot of people..." her voice fading.

By the way she emphasized the word "see," Aidan concluded that it meant more than just seeing someone for a coffee.

"Okay. I think I get your drift. Men or women?"

The woman twitched and stared at him as if he had just said something shocking.

"I mean— is he hetero or gay? Or bi? Given that you're looking for him here, I thought...?

Her strong reaction had thrown him a little off balance. At last, she answered.

"We don't really socialize like that. I mean, party and things like that. He likes it, but I don't. We don't really talk much about it either. But I think he's into both."

For a short second, Aidan thought he saw her cringe but thought to himself it was probably just out of worry for her friend. It seemed a bit odd that close friends would not know each other's sexual orientation. Love, sex, and romance felt like all he ever talked about with Drew. On the other hand, he wouldn't mind being spared some of the details Drew usually provided. Sometimes it was a bit much. Images he would have preferred not to have stuck in his mind. It might not be a bad idea to leave some things untold. The woman's friendship with this man, Seb, was probably based on some other mutual interest. He wondered what that might be but refrained from asking.

"So, what makes you think he might be here? Do you know if he was meeting this person he saw here, or does he just come here a lot?"

"No, I don't know anything, really. As I said, we don't talk much about it, but I think he's mentioned this place, or I might have overheard him talking about it with someone on the phone. Either way, it was the first place that came to mind when I decided to start looking for him. Unfortunately, the staff hasn't been very helpful." She made a face and glanced over at the bar.

To a degree, Aidan understood the bartender's reluctance to talk. Some people might not want to get found, and, for historical reasons, if nothing else, it was understandable not wanting to risk outing people. Still, this woman was clearly worried out of her mind, and it couldn't have hurt to show her some goodwill—the woman whose name he did not even know.

"Aidan."

He extended his hand for a handshake.

"Marie."

She put a surprisingly cool and thin hand in his for a short moment. The grip was stronger than he would have anticipated. At that very moment, Drew returned from the dancefloor, accompanied by another man.

"Nice to see you're not wasting your time." Drew rolled his eyes before introducing himself to Marie. "Drew. And this is Mogge." He did a little salutation in the direction of the other man and scurried off to the bar.

The Swedes' ability to come up with ugly nicknames never ceased to amaze Aidan. To his relief, Mogge extended his hand and presented himself with his full name.

"Morgan Lundin."

He had a warm and firm handshake. After they had all introduced themselves, Aidan invited Morgan to take a seat at the table.

"Would you mind helping us out with something?"

Aidan was eager to show Marie that he was a capable investigator. When Morgan had seated himself comfortably, he nodded and looked at them with curiosity. Aidan turned to Marie and pointed to her phone. She immediately took the hint and held it up so that Morgan could see.

"I'm sorry for being so forward, but would you happen to know this man?"

Morgan looked surprised at first, but when he inspected the photo closer, a smile spread across his face. Jokingly he raised his arms in defeat.

"Guilty."

Aidan gave Marie, who showed no sign of a reaction, a quick glance before he got back to his questioning.

"Oh, really? Do you know him well? When did you last see him?"

"Well, why do you ask?" Morgan suddenly looked a little suspicious.

This caused Marie to cut into the conversation.

"I'm a close friend of his. I mean, not like that..." She struggled to find the right word but gave up trying when she saw that Morgan understood what she meant. "He has gone missing. I haven't heard from him in a week, and we're usually in touch every day. And he hasn't been to his office either. I'm really worried about him."

Aidan noticed a shred of concern in Morgan's eyes.

"Are you serious? I'm sorry, that sucks. I'll tell you anything I know, even though it's not that much."

Drew came back from the bar with four beers and a brilliant smile. Aidan hadn't even had a first sip of the beer he already had in front of him. But instead of pointing that out, he gave Drew, who would then realize that he was expected to keep his mouth shut, for the time being, the rundown on the situation.

"We had a relationship of sorts." Morgan continued. "Not love or anything like that, purely sexual. We met here for the first time, actually. He wasn't here for the music, if you know what I mean. I took him home, and since then, we've hooked up from time to time. Either at my place or hotels. To be honest, I don't even know where he lives."

"When was the last time you saw him?"

"About three weeks ago, I think, I've been away on vacation. I texted him when I got back last Sunday. He never wrote me back, but I didn't think anything of it."

"So, you haven't had any contact at all in the last three weeks?"

"That's right. I kind of expected him to get back to me sooner or later. But now I have other things on my mind." Morgan gave Drew a knowing look. Drew, who didn't speak Swedish and hadn't understood a word of the conversation, returned the look with a flirtatious smile and put his hand on Morgan's arm. "Honestly, I wouldn't be too worried about him. He knows how to take care of himself."

"Do you know if there were others?"

"Yes, god, yes! He's an insatiable little rascal, that one. But I think I ranked pretty high on his list. He gave me this."

He stretched his fingers down the collar of his exclusive, tailor-made, light gray shirt. When his hand found what it was looking for, he presented them with a small piece of jewelry, a little silver angel on a necklace.

"He told me I'm his angel because I give him what he needs."

Aidan glanced over at Marie, worried that this information was more than she was wanted to hear. However, she was either completely unaffected by what they had just been told or very good at keeping a straight face. When Aidan heard Drew offer to be Morgan's angel, he decided to leave the two men alone for now and redirected his attention towards Marie.

"It may not be much, but at least now we know that he's a regular here."

As he said the word, *we*, he realized that there was a possibility that Marie would take issue with him, including himself, in her search. He studied her face for a reaction, but she still did not show any visible emotion of any kind.

"I once got a necklace like that." Her eyes were gazing

down at the table again, and she had this vacant look, almost as if she was talking to herself. "I'm his angel too..." she trailed off.

Aidan was still struggling hard to read her without any success. She smiled faintly. He wasn't sure if it was melancholy or sarcasm, and soon the moment was over.

"I should probably go home. I'm beat." She looked at Aidan. "Thank you for helping me out. It really means a lot."

"Oh, it's nothing. Here." He reached into his back pocket. "Take my card. It's for my other business, soccer coaching. But my number is on there. Give me a call if you want to meet up tomorrow or something and figure out the next step for the investigation."

As soon as he had finished the sentence, he got the feeling that he was getting entangled in a web of deceit. The phrase "my other business" clearly implied that private investigations was his main business. He was well aware that the assignments he had been given, things like driving Gunvor around and trying to make sense of her findings, hardly qualified him to call himself an investigator. When it came to fieldwork, his own merits were limited to keeping eyes on a woman in a nightclub, an attempt to assist Gunvor on her last case, and then, almost immediately, losing sight of her. When Gunvor had eventually cracked the case, with David and Elin's help, he had been off coaching at a soccer camp for a Manchester youth team. But then, Aidan thought, if Marie wanted to see him again, there would be opportunities, in time, to tell her that his main occupation was actually neither as a private investigator nor a soccer coach, but as an English teacher.

" Okay, thanks."

At least, she did not object. Her cool lips touched his cheek lightly before she stood up and raised her hand in a farewell.

CHAPTER 3
THURSDAY, OCTOBER 29

MOGGE COULDN'T HELP but throw all his principles about public displays of affection out the window. All he wanted was to kiss this wonderful man and for this moment to go on forever. But as the conductor of the Arlanda Express train, for the second time, and this time with an amused tone in his voice, shouted out the last call over the PA, their lips finally parted.

Drew remained standing just behind the doors as they closed, and when they were securely shut, he put his palm to the window in what he hoped would come across as a meaningful gesture. Mogge responded by putting his own hand on his side of the window, ending up in sort of a high five divided by half an inch of glass. They looked deep into each other's eyes, and they both knew that they would meet again soon. It was already agreed. But at this moment, Friday night was a lifetime away. When the train started moving, Mogge followed on the platform for as long as he could before he let his hand slide off the window. Long after the train had disappeared in the distance, he just stood there on the platform, looking after it. It wasn't until the next train approached the station that he finally collected himself.

Mogge strolled back to his central apartment on Grev Turegatan. All he could think about was Drew. That magical night they had spent together. He had quickly become drunk with love and tried to convince Drew to stay a while longer. Drew had, in turn, assured him he really wanted nothing more but had to return to London for work. Until the very last moment, they had remained in each other's arms. As a result, their breakfast had been reduced to a cup of coffee that they had to drink on foot while they hurried down to the train station. During the walk, Drew had asked him to come to visit him over the weekend. Mogge had immediately agreed. He was already counting down the hours.

Despite not having gotten much in the way of sleep that night, his plan was to get as much work as humanly possible out of the way in one day and then delegate whatever he could to his employees. That way, he could keep the business afloat while just putting in a few hours a day for the next couple of weeks, working remotely from London. He hadn't mentioned anything to Drew yet. They had only discussed the weekend. As much as Mogge did not want to come off as pushy or too forward, judging from their emotional farewell, he felt pretty confident that Drew would not take issue with his plan.

Unable to resist the urge, he grabbed the phone from his pocket and typed out the text,

Miss you...

It didn't take long for a reply to appear on the screen.

Longing for you...

He enjoyed his walk back to the apartment—his thoughts filled by Drew. The air was cold, but he enjoyed it. A new day. Hopefully, a new beginning.

He got the elevator to the third floor. His floor. Still caught up in thoughts, he fiddled with the keys for a bit before managing to open the door. As usual, he left the door slightly open while taking off his shoes and coat. But then the routine was disturbed. Suddenly there was someone else in the hallway. Someone who must have followed him—who entered through the door after him?

He noticed the raincoat that seemed too big—wondering what this person was doing here.

"Excuse me, can I help..."

He was brutally interrupted when the intruder lifted their hand over their head. Something flashed—an axe.

Tearing stabs came in rapid succession, one after another. Unbearable pain. He wanted to scream. To make it stop. He was supposed to go to London. He had just met the love of his life, for god's sake. But he couldn't make a sound, and he couldn't make it stop. When the world faded around him, he was still thinking about Drew.

CHAPTER 4

IT WAS a warm and somewhat stale apartment that greeted Gunvor back from her trip. There was no doubt about the fact that it had been abandoned for over a month. She took a quick look around the two-room apartment and concluded that her neighbor, a friend, had successfully kept her lemon tree and all the plants in the kitchen window alive. When her eyes fell on a bottle of red wine on the kitchen table, she smiled. Tucked under the bottle was a welcome home note from Aidan. Gunvor sent him a grateful thought, but she felt a sting of disappointment at the same time. She had hoped, well, actually more or less expected, that he would be there to greet her in person.

They had not seen each other since he went away to Manchester, six weeks earlier to the day. After that, she had, together with Elin and David, suffered through the most dreadful day and night. David had witnessed a murder. Elin had been kidnapped, and Gunvor herself had also been captured. It had not taken her too long to put her trauma behind her. After all, she was a private investigator and well aware of the risks of the job. However, the feelings of guilt from bringing her young friends Elin and David into the whole mess were harder to move past. Her beloved partner, Kjell, had comforted her again and again by telling her that they were grown up enough to make their own decisions, while at the same time, making sure to point out that he thought Gunvor should make some life changes. He did love her for who she was. But he had come to realize that her new line of work was not at all as safe as Gunvor had first led him to believe. Kjell was a retired firefighter who was now living a life of leisure on Gran Canaria, patiently waiting for Gunvor to wrap up her career and join him.

When they first met, hand tremors had recently put an abrupt end to Gunvor's successful career as a chief surgeon. He had been sympathetic with her unwillingness to be forced into early retirement by a mild physical condition. However, after a year of this new occupation of her's, that was clearly both dangerous and mentally taxing, he could not help but think that it would be better for Gunvor to let go of her ambitions. He wished she would settle for a comfortable life with him in the Canary sun. To his disappointment, Gunvor did not share his view, at least not quite yet. So, when Manuel from the agency called with a new case, she had booked a one-way flight back to Stockholm.

Aidan and Gunvor had spoken many times over the phone during her stay on Gran Canaria. But she had looked forward to breathing new life into the story, in person, and answering all of Aidan's questions, accompanied by their customary bottle of red wine.

It was already late in the evening when she uncorked the bottle and poured its contents into her favorite glass. Starting the next day, she told herself, she would begin a healthier lifestyle. She had planned to do that the previous month when she arrived at Kjell's house in Arguineguin, but under some mysterious circumstances, they had ended up sharing a bottle of red wine with almost every dinner. Usually followed up with a digestif on the terrace, while enjoying the last warmth of the sun. After dinner, they had not been able to resist ending the night with another glass of wine in the warm breeze, listening to the quiet roar of the ocean from the darkness below.

October was coming to an end. For the people of Stockholm, that meant enjoying an evening on the balcony was nothing more than a distant memory. Instead, Gunvor put a couple of deep red candles in the holders she had gotten at last year's Christmas bazaar at a nearby art college. Soon she felt at peace, even without the company she desired.

She finished the bottle alone. By the time it was half empty, it only made sense to drink the rest of it. That way, she could start her new healthy lifestyle in the morning. Or maybe the day after that. Good, clean living.

While enjoying the last sips, she went over her plans for the next day. There was an appointment scheduled in the morning and a briefing with Manuel and the new client. Manuel was the chief and the founder of her agency. But he was also a force to be reckoned with when out in the field. He put his life on the line during Gunvor's last case. For that, she would be eternally grateful. However, in a strange twist of fate, in the end, if it hadn't been for David and her, things could have gotten ugly for him. Luckily, it had all turned out for the better, and in the end, the incident had fortified their relationship.

In the evening, she had also invited Elin and David over for dinner. That meant that she would need to take some time during the day to restock her kitchen, which was now empty after the trip. She looked forward to finally seeing them again. They had only been in touch a few times, and very briefly, while she had been away. The drama of the last case had left them all in need of some time apart to process everything that had gone down. But now she was excited for them all to get back together.

When Gunvor, at last, crawled into bed, she pondered over what could have been so important that it kept Aidan from giving her a proper welcome back. They knew each other well. At least, she had thought she knew everything there was to know about his routines and habits. The note puzzled her.

Welcome home. Busy, so see you later. I left you some coffee, milk, and veggie quiche.

Not that it was anything weird about the note itself, but it was uncharacteristic of him not to specify what was keeping him busy. He had gone through all the effort to bring her food and water the plants. Surely, he could have taken the time to add one more sentence to the note, explaining what he was doing.

CHAPTER 5

EVEN THOUGH AIDAN had been feeling a little nervous all day, it was with some excitement that he walked through the front doors of Café Rival, where he and Marie had arranged to meet. A few hours earlier, when he woke up, abandoned by the warm glow of the alcohol that had soothed him the night before, he had doubted that he would ever see or hear from her again. But to his surprise and delight, the phone buzzed with a text from Marie, asking if he would be available for a meeting that same evening. He agreed without hesitation, though he could feel the sting of a bad conscience regarding Gunvor. They hadn't seen each other for a long time, and he knew that he was probably expected to be her welcoming committee.

On the other hand, there was plenty of time to catch up now that she would be back at home for a while. To compensate for neglecting her, he made her the quiche he knew she liked and picked up a bottle of decent wine. She would probably be alright for one night.

Aidan had tried looking up Marie online. After all, he didn't know anything about her and was interested in any info he could get. However, with only a first name to go on, the number she had texted from was an unregistered pay as you go SIM card. The attempt had been futile.

He had barely admitted it to himself, but one of the main reasons he had done the online search was to see if she was single or in a relationship. For all he knew, she could even have a family. He had only assumed that she was single based on the fact that she had been out looking for her friend on her own. At the same time, he was well aware that many married couples live almost entirely separate lives. He decided that he would make a subtle inquiry when they met. After all, it could be useful for the investigation.

Marie had already seated herself in one of the corners of the café with a sandwich and a jug of coffee in front of her. Slumped down on the couch like that, beneath the spearmint-colored walls covered in photos of local icons, she appeared much smaller than he remembered her. Maybe it was the fragile look in her eyes or the weariness she radiated. Her whole being seemed to ooze of abandonment.

Aidan shook her hand and hung his coat on the chair opposite her before he went to make his order at the counter. He had not been able to resist eating some of the quiche that he made for Gunvor before heading out, so he decided to settle for a lager, hoping Marie would not find it weird that he ordered alcohol for a meeting.

"Any new developments?" It seemed like a redundant question, but he could not think of a better opening.

"No."

Despite the strained look on her face, Aidan could not get over how pretty her eyes were, shaped like almonds. The irises had sprinkles of grey on a green backdrop. He really had to make an effort to stay on topic. Luckily, he had a little speech prepared. Before he began, he took a couple of swigs of beer in an attempt to calm his nerves and the throbbing headache, an after-effect from the night before.

"Okay, how about this?" He paused for effect and grabbed a pen and a notebook from the brand-new shoulder bag he had bought at Tiger of Sweden a few days earlier. It was a little expensive, but he had not treated himself to something this nice in a long time. It was just so comfortable, and it really made him look sharp.

"I would like you to tell me everything you know about Seb. How well does he know you? What do you two do together when you see him? What does he get up to when you're not together? How often do you see him? Things like that. If I have some information, I can put together a profile, which will make it much easier to find him." Aidan had been trying to remember the process he had seen Gunvor use when she pieced together fragments of information to get the full scope of a case. The idea was to get a sense of what a missing person was or was not likely to do. Based on that, you could conclude whether the disappearance had been voluntary or not, and where they might have ended up.

Marie gave him a puzzled look before she gazed out the window overlooking Mariatorget and cleared her throat.

"A profile? Well—I suppose it has been a bit strenuous at times. In a way, we're like an old couple. We've known each other for a long time. Since high school. We were inseparable back then—went to a lot of parties." She smiled, but it was a smile filled with melancholy. "We were regulars at all the hip clubs back then. Always on the guest lists of Big Brother, After Dark, Ritz… what's the name of that place again…? Well, never mind. No, wait, Confetti. Was it Confetti?" She trailed off, apparently deep in thought.

Aidan had passed thirty by the time he moved to Sweden and had never heard of any of these places but made sure to scribble down all names in his notebook.

"All the partying got more and more intense up to a point when we were out almost every day. I got bored with that lifestyle pretty quickly, but he still carries on. Seb has never been one to gossip, and I haven't really been interested in hearing about it, so I know almost nothing about that part of his life now." Marie continued to stare out the window as she spoke. The gentle autumn rain created little pools of water in the street. She sighed, just barely audible. "We share our own world when we're together. That's enough for me."

"How often do you see him?"

She seemed to consider the fairly simple question for a surprisingly long time before she answered.

"He works a lot. I see him from time-to-time when he's free."

"How often would that be, if you were to make an estimation?"

"A few times a week, maybe?"

"And you say he spends a lot of time at work. Where does he work?"

"That's not important. I've already spoken with his co-workers. They haven't heard anything from him. I don't want you calling them."

Aidan shrugged. It was her friend, so it seemed fair to let her make the calls.

"Does he have any favorite places that might be worth staking out? Any restaurants or anything like that? Maybe someplace you used to go together?"

She shook her head. For a moment, he thought she was going to burst into tears, but suddenly something changed in her expression. The sadness was gone, and she gave Aidan a stern look.

"Now listen. I don't want to spread any gossip about him. He's my friend, and he trusts me. I don't want to break that trust. And honestly, I don't see why you would need to make a profile of him. I already know him, and besides, we have the photo to show around. If you really want to help, I would be grateful for any suggestions of places where someone like him might go to party. As I said, I don't really go out anymore."

All this secrecy was a little disappointing to Aidan, but he was glad that she at least had admitted that she wanted his help.

"Absolutely. I know most of the gay bars in this town. That's where we're looking, right?

She nodded.

"So, where do we start?"

CHAPTER 6
FRIDAY, OCTOBER 30

GUNVOR GOT UP EARLY and well-rested, despite having stayed up pretty late the night before. The weeks spent on Gran Canaria had replenished her energy, and she felt eager to take on this new case. After what had happened on the last one, it had been a blessing to be able just to take off and get a change of scenery. Things had come very close to a tragic outcome, and if anything bad had happened to Elin or David, it would have been on her. That was something that had lingered with her and could not be soothed by the praise she had received from the police and the media. They had caught a murderer and exposed a trafficking ring, but they had put a lot, maybe too much, on the line doing it. Luckily, the warm sandy beaches and tepid water of the Gran Canaria had rubbed off the sharpest edges of the trauma and her bad conscience.

She immediately recognized the discreet knock on the door. They had come up with it together. Loud enough to be audible, but quiet enough that it would not wake someone who was asleep. She opened the door with a happy smile and invited Aidan in for a cup of fresh coffee from the new Aero-Press she had brought home with her.

As they sat down by the kitchen table, Gunvor noticed that something was different about him, but she could not put her finger on what it was. He had always been adventurous and funny, with a twinkle in his eyes, but this was something else. Something new.

"Drew came to visit the other day."

"Oh, that's nice! Is he still here?"

"No, no. He just spent the day. Or spent the night, rather. Well, not with me, obviously. He had just been dumped, but he found a new bloke here in about ten minutes, so tragedy averted, I guess."

"He certainly has a talent for making the most of life." Gunvor chuckled. "And he left you alone at some bar, I assume?"

"How did you know?" Aidan smiled too. "That's alright, though. We ended up at a place with a nice bar and good music. Actually, something quite strange happened." Aidan made a theatrical pause to make sure he had Gunvor's full attention before he went on. "A woman came up to me with a picture of some guy. Apparently, a close friend of hers that has gone missing. I told her I have a little experience with missing persons investigations."

He looked at Gunvor for a reaction, but she did not say anything.

"Anyway, at first she thought he'd just met someone and would turn up. But then, as days passed, she started getting worried, and when she called his office, they let her know that he hasn't been in all week. So, because I know most of the gay bars in the city, thanks to Drew, I offered to help look for him. We had a meeting yesterday to come up with a plan."

When Gunvor heard this explanation of why he had not been waiting home to greet her back from her trip the day before, it all made sense. Even though he did not have her experience, she knew that he shared her passion for thrills and mystery. Still, she could not help but worry about him. Aidan did not seem the least bit concerned about the seriousness of the situation he had just laid out to her, as he sat there with a faint smile on his lips. She was not sure if he was just excited about the mission, or if there was something else at play.

"What do the police make of it?"

"I'm not sure. Marie just told me that he'd been reported missing, not much else. She seems very secretive."

The sparkle in his eyes dampened a little.

"Right. I suppose they're likely to put a case like this on the backburner anyway since no crime has been reported. Has Missing Persons been informed?"

"I don't think she wants to make a big deal out of it. I guess that's why she's out looking on her own."

"Well, she's not alone anymore, is she?"

"I try to be helpful wherever I can. And I do actually know one or two things about private investigations these days." Aidan gave Gunvor a meaningful nod. "Thanks to you."

"You're a good man. Just let me know if you need any help, okay? I'm sure the agency will take on the case too if she feels like she can afford it."

"Thanks, but I think we're good for now. Maybe if we manage to find out some details about the final hours before his disappearance, we're going for a big bar crawl tonight. Hopefully, I'll get some people to talk. The plan is for me to pretend to be a concerned lover of his."

Gunvor contemplated this idea while Aidan went on to recap the rest of his night out with Drew. She admired Aidan's eagerness to help out a stranger, even though it was now beyond any doubt that he had taken an interest in this Marie. She was, however, not convinced that he was the right man for the job. True, he had been indispensable to her in the past. But that had been in the role of a brainstorming partner. He did not have much in the way of field experience. Even their young friends Elin and David had seen more real action. She calmed herself by thinking that, after all, the police had been informed, and Aidan's commitment to help must have been a significant psychological relief for Marie. Maybe this was not such a bad way for him to gain a little experience.

"I'm in a bit of a hurry. I've got to teach a class in a minute."

Aidan got up to rinse the coffee cups when his phone buzzed. He immediately put the cup down next to the sink, and Gunvor noticed that he reached for the phone with unusual eagerness. After reading the text, he looked a little disappointed.

"It's Drew," he said with his eyes still locked on the phone. "That Morgan bloke didn't turn out to be so great after all. He was supposed to come to London today, but it seems like he ghosted."

"Oh, that's too bad. I suppose it wasn't meant to be. At least he cheered him up."

"He seems anything but cheerful now." Aidan got back to the dishes with a troubled look. "Drew must have really thought this guy was something special."

"Wait a minute, didn't you just say he was supposed to go to London today? It's still early in the morning; maybe he's just having trouble with his phone or getting off work or something?

"That's true. It's still a little sketchy not to get in touch if you miss your flight, but if he's anything like Drew...." He picked up the phone without finishing his statement and began to write back. Gunvor got up to take over the now-abandoned task of rinsing the cups before walking Aidan to the door.

"You be careful now with your investigation. Remember that you don't know why this person is missing. Worst case, someone wants him to stay missing, and if that's the case well, it might be best not to get in the way."

"Don't worry. I got it."

Gunvor restrained herself from saying anything more on the subject.

"Alright, then. Let me know when you're available for dinner and gossip."

"Will do."

Gunvor sat back down at the kitchen table for a minute after locking the door behind Aidan. She was happy for him that he finally met someone. He had been alone for many years now. She just hoped it would not be at the cost of their friendship. If this Marie was someone she would also grow to like, would that not be nice? New friends did not exactly grow on trees in her life. She thought about this for a moment, then sighed at her tendency always to get ahead of herself.

CHAPTER 7

MANUEL, Gaston, and Frida all greeted Gunvor with hugs as soon as she arrived at the agency. She had taken an earlier train to make sure she would have some time to catch up with her colleagues before the meeting. Even though she was not a full-time member of the team, she had gotten to know and grow fond of all three of them. Especially Manuel, with whom she had spent hours on the phone, dissecting and trying to make sense of her last case, on her holiday in Gran Canaria. He looked neat in the dark blue suit that was almost annoyingly well fitted on his athletic body. His dark hair had grown longer since they last met. Aside from that, he looked like his usual self with a warm smile and lively, brown eyes.

Frida had gotten rid of most of her long blonde hair. Somehow though, this new look only made her even more feminine. However, in contrast to her frail appearance, she was actually a fearless and forceful adventurer. She had spent years on the national taskforce before becoming a private investigator.

Gaston looked much younger than his age. With his baggy

jeans and oversize hoodie, you could easily have mistaken him for a teen, even though he was almost thirty years old. Before the client finally rang the doorbell, he told Gunvor, with adorable pride, that he and his wife were expecting their first child.

"Time for you to get a real job, then." Frida teased as she went to open the front door.

As soon as the client walked in, they all quieted down and did their best to appear serious and professional. Manuel and Gunvor shook hands with the woman, who presented herself as Eva Cedergren, and showed her into the conference room. Manuel took care of her elegant, bone-white woolen coat as she and Gunvor each took their seats.

"I know we've gone over some of the details on the phone," Manuel began as he made himself comfortable in his chair. "But if it's all the same to you, it would be great to hear the whole story from the beginning. Gunvor here will handle the case, so she needs to hear everything firsthand from you."

Gunvor observed Eva as she began talking. She looked about fifty years old with lovely, thick but not coarse, copper hair that ended just below her shoulders. Her slightly freckled face was almost perfectly symmetrical. She wore a grey polo with a black skirt and a pink lipstick that accented her striking natural beauty.

Even though Gunvor was aware that she had been blessed with a pleasing appearance herself and was very fit for her age, her aching knees and the inevitable wrinkles had become a constant reminder of her aging. Compared to this creature, she could not help feeling old and bleak. She had considered putting on full makeup, but lately, she thought that only made her look even older. It was as if makeup highlighted the wrinkles rather than concealing them. Instead, she had settled for a burgundy red lipstick and sober clothing – a white shirt, a black skirt, and a jacket.

"My husband has gone missing."

Eva opened her purse and dug up a photo, which she then handed over. Gunvor inspected the picture carefully. She thought the man in it seemed to emit false authority and self-conceit. It was the kind of portrait she had grown to despise during her career as a surgeon. During her training, she had been thrilled by the thought of helping others, being surrounded by like-minded peers who had chosen the field of work to do good. Instead, she had soon found herself in a dubious hierarchy filled with rivalry, backstabbing, and bullying. More often than not, portraits of this kind, touched up to the point that it made the real subject look like a cheap copy, would decorate the chief physicians' desks. She had to restrain herself to keep from letting her contempt show.

"I haven't heard from him in a week. I've been in touch with his office, and they told me he has taken a leave of absence. That's why I've come to you rather than the police."

Gunvor decided that any attempt at comforting would not likely be appreciated. Eva seemed like a person who valued her privacy. Just coming here was likely a challenge to her pride. Gunvor found herself wondering whether she wanted to locate her husband because she was actually worried for him or if she just wanted a chance to tell him off to his face. Not that it was any of her business. When it was her turn to speak, she did so in a dry, professional tone that did not carry any trace of her contemplations.

"I see. Would you mind telling me his name, place of work, when he disappeared, and for how long he has requested the leave?"

"His name is Per Cedergren. He works for his father's company. Shipowners. High-end luxury cruises. Per is one of the three people working directly under his father, and he stands to inherit the business once his father decides to step back. But for now, he is not being cut any slack. Let me tell you that." She made a face to show her disapproval before she went on. "The last time I saw him was a week ago, as I just told you, so Friday the 23rd. He was heading out to our summerhouse. We have a cabin in the archipelago. He had a lot of work to catch up on and needed some peace and quiet, nothing unusual. He was due back on Sunday evening but never showed up, obviously. And I haven't been able to reach him on his phone or anything like that."

Eva had a calm and matter of fact expression on her face while she spoke, and her eyes were locked on Gunvor as if Manuel was not even in the room.

"Eventually, I called his work. He has been granted two weeks off as per his request."

Gunvor thought she saw her flinch, but it was over so quickly that it was hard to decide whether it had actually happened. Eva's eyes were still fixed on hers. They seemed to demand an answer of some kind. Gunvor hesitated for a moment.

"Did you see it coming?"

Without turning away, Eva let out a sigh.

"No. I really don't understand this at all. He's the love of my life, and we've been together since forever. I think maybe he's depressed. He has struggled with depression in the past. I'm worried that he's sad and lonely somewhere and can't see a way out. He's always under a lot of pressure from work. The amount of money they're handling on a day-to-day basis is enormous, and even though it's a family business, it doesn't take more than a tiny mistake to get in serious trouble with the board."

A tear ran down her left cheek. No face, no sobs. Just a single tear.

"Or maybe it's actually because it's a family business."

Eva smiled vaguely at Gunvor's comment. They went on talking for a little while, but Gunvor was not able to get much more useful information out of her. Apparently, there was nothing unusual about them spending some time apart. Per often worked late nights and weekends at the company his father had built up from the ground. Eva had given up her career once they got married. Gunvor could not understand how anyone could put themselves in a situation like that, being completely dependent on someone. She knew that she, at least, would not have been able to stand a life without working and feeling useful. What would even be the reason to get out of bed in the morning?

Eva told them that Per had to attend a lot of business dinners, but she had stopped going with him a long time ago. Instead, they spent time together whenever he was off work. Often in their summerhouse. That was where Per was supposedly heading the last time Eva had seen him. She did not think he would still be there. She said she was not even sure that he had really gone there. Over the weekend, they had only communicated via texts. It was hard to get a good signal out there, so they had installed a landline for the house. She had tried calling the number several times over the week, but no-one had picked up. Eva thought this was enough proof that the house stood empty. Gunvor was not convinced by the argument. He had not replied to any of her texts either since Sunday, so the only thing that seemed obvious was that Per either could not or was not interested in getting in touch.

After some negotiating, Eva reluctantly gave Gunvor a key and permission to check the house. This was a relief for Gunvor, as there did not seem to be much else to go on. She thought that Per might well still be there. Or perhaps on some Caribbean island with some young vixen. He seemed to have enough money to be able to charter a private jet and just vanish, should he want to. However, to assume that he had disappeared without a trace and leave the investigation at that would be professional misconduct. She wrote down his social security number and any other personal data Eva was willing to share, and with that, the meeting was concluded. They shook hands and agreed that they would keep each other updated. Gunvor asked Gaston to check with the travel agencies and see if there were any flight records for a Per Cedergren before heading off to Per's office.

CHAPTER 8

CARL CEDERGREN WAS a man of stature in his early seventies. It did not take more than a single glance at Per's father to realize that he was someone used to being in charge. He wore an ash-colored three-piece suit that was clearly expensive, and the shirt under it had a hint of coral that emphasized his tan, which in turn accentuated his bright white smile. He was obviously putting a lot of effort and money into his appearance. Gunvor thought he had probably made some surgical adjustments and lifts as well. She had never been a fan of plastic surgery being used for vanity; she knew all too well from her own years at the hospital that the skills of these expert surgeons were sorely needed elsewhere. But looking at Carl, she could not help thinking that at least he had spent his money well.

His secretary had been very helpful, and despite not having booked an appointment, it did not take more than a couple of minutes before she was let into his office. Carl greeted her in the doorway with a solid handshake and invited her to take a seat. The enormous corner office was furnished with a great pyramid mahogany desk, a lounge suite, and a conference table that would fit at least eight people. Windows from floor to ceiling overlooked the islets Kastellholmen and Skeppsholmen in the very heart of the city.

"How can I be of service?" Carl carried an expression of friendly curiosity.

"I'm looking for your son, actually, Per Cedergren. I take it you've been informed of his disappearance. You don't happen to know anything about his whereabouts?"

Carl gazed out the windows for a moment before he answered. Gunvor thought she could see a hint of amusement on his face, but it was hard to tell for sure.

"He's on a little vacation. He'll be back soon enough."

"Do you know where? He has failed to tell his wife of this vacation. She's very worried."

"I don't know where he is."

Gunvor looked at him in silence, waiting for him to say more. Manuel had taught her that silence often is a better tool, for making people talk, than questions.

"I didn't know about his plans either. He apparently couldn't be bothered to let us know even a day ahead that he'd be gone for the whole week, and the next one. Highly inappropriate if you ask me. We're trying to run a business here, for god's sake. But it is what it is. I suppose he has his reasons."

"Do you have any theories as to what that reason might be?"

Carl had a conflicted look on his face and seemed unsure whether to answer the question.

"I really couldn't tell you. If you want me to venture a guess, I'd say some men have greater needs than others."

"You mean he's off cheating on his wife?"

When she saw his frown, she quickly added.

"You must excuse my straightforwardness. I'm not here to judge. I just want to know whether he's safe or not."

"As I said, I don't know anything for sure. But that would be my assumption, yes. My son and I are birds of a feather. I know what a long marriage like that can do to you. He's never confided much in me, but it's clear that he spends a lot of his nights out and about. The way I see it, as long as he's not screwing up his work, it's none of my business. Besides, I've never heard his wife complain about it before."

"Has he ever disappeared like this in the past?"

"Never, and it won't happen again. Not if he wants to take over this company one day."

"And I assume that you haven't been in contact with him since he called in on Monday."

"That is correct."

"Alright, then. I'm not here to pass judgment and tell anyone how to live their lives. Besides, I'm a divorcee myself. I just hope you're right and that he will show up soon, but the fact is that he has broken his pattern with this "vacation" and has left his wife worried and upset. So, I'm obliged to keep looking. I would be very grateful if you agreed to let me know if you hear anything from him."

"That, I will do." Carl stood up and extended his hand for a goodbye.

On her way over to the grocery store, she went over the whole conversation in her head. A picture of Per Cedergren was slowly forming in her head. A man accustomed to money and influence, to getting what he wanted, a beautiful wife—yet restless. It seemed tragic that his wife would not even suspect infidelity. Could you really live that closely with someone and not notice something like that?

CHAPTER 9

"OH, dear children! You don't know how happy I am to see you!" Gunvor stretched her arms toward Elin and David.

"The Fruängen Bureau, if I may..." The rest of David's protest was smothered as his mouth was pressed into Gunvor's shoulder when she embraced them both. She had been looking forward to this moment. David's comment reminded her of the late summer afternoon on Aidan's balcony when they had decided to pursue the last case even after the client had withdrawn the request. That afternoon they had not been able to imagine just how dangerous the mission would turn out to be. Sitting on that balcony, drinking elderflower juice, joking about how they needed a name for the team.

"How have you been? Missed me?"

When she took a step back to give her guests some room to get their coats off, she noted how stylish Elin looked. Elin, who usually showed up in sweatpants and without any makeup, seemed to have taken to the look they had developed for her when she had to fit into the nightclubs they had been staking out. Gunvor cracked a smile when she saw the confidence and pride that now radiated from Elin. The difference was truly staggering.

Gunvor had cursed herself for bringing nothing but chaos and trauma into Elin's life. Seeing her like this was a huge weight off her chest. She was clearly not in need of anyone's pity and concern. On the contrary, she seemed to have made it out of the experience blooming.

There was no doubt that David, too, had gone through a transformation. From an insufferable teenager, hanging out with his friends on the street corner, shouting insults to passersby, he had become a tolerable, if not polite, and confident young man. His exterior had not changed as dramatically as Elin's, but he did look considerably more like a grown-up than when they had first met, less than a year before.

"It's been good to have some time to process everything that happened. But it's really good to see you." Elin gave Gunvor a wide smile as she said this and then turned to David. "And you too."

"You two haven't kept in touch?" Gunvor was surprised. Even if you did not plan for it, Fruängen was a small enough place that you were bound to run into the people you knew regularly.

"We have, but she's only hanging out with Chibbe these days." David gave Elin a teasing smile. Chibbe had been one of the suspects in the case but had, in the end, assisted them in solving it.

"Well, excuse me, but you're the one spending all your time with Bella and your precious studies." Elin rolled her eyes and did her best to look offended.

"So, things are going well with Chibbe?" Gunvor cut in. "And who's this Bella then? And what are you studying?" She poured wine into their glasses and motioned to her guests to help themselves to the chili.

"Well?"

"That's a lot of questions at once, even for a PI. Can we go one at a time, please?" David teased. "I got into the security officer's training program."

"Hey, good for you. Congratulations." In just a few months' time, Gunvor was pleasantly surprised that he had gone from making a hobby out of pestering security guards to now being on his way to becoming one himself.

"With the end goal of becoming a detective, of course." He was proud of his effort, and even his friends had been reluctantly impressed though they had done their best not to show it. "Or perhaps a bodyguard."

"I'll say, you two really get up to all sorts of things when I'm not around. Why don't you just get your grades done and apply to the police academy right away?"

"That's what I said!" Elin nodded eagerly.

"I know, but... can't you just be happy for me, that I've done this?" David had a crestfallen look on his face.

"But we are! I'm happy and proud of you for getting your act together. I just want you to realize that you can go far." She hadn't meant to come off as discouraging or thinking that security guard training wasn't good enough. Being a person that had always put her career first, the truth was she didn't think it was quite good enough. Anyone could become a security guard, and she did not want David to waste his potential. On the other hand, she did not want to belittle his improvements either. She was aware that this was a big step for him.

"I have to start somewhere, don't I?"

"Of course you do. We're proud of you, David."

"Yes, you're doing great."

With that, David was back in a good mood.

"So, are you going to tell me about this—Bella?" Gunvor was eager to get up to speed on everything that had been going on since she had been away.

"Oh, it's just a girl I met when we staked out Sturehof after Elin was taken. She's really sweet and everything, but it has sort of petered out."

"He said she's too vain." Elin cut in and turned to Gunvor. "There's something you'd never expected to hear from David, isn't it?"

Gunvor was not able to hold back a laugh. Elin was right. Not long ago, she had not been sure he even knew the meaning of the word.

"She is, though! I can't spend my days bothering about who's wearing ugly shoes or getting their hair cut at the wrong salon or didn't get into this or that nightclub."

"Alright, alright." Gunvor chuckled. "How are things with Chibbe, then?" She turned her attention towards Elin.

"Kind of the same thing, actually." Her eyes flickered between Gunvor and David before she continued. It was obvious that she and David had discussed the matter, and she was seeking his countenance. He nodded lightly.

"Not that he's talking about shoes all day." She giggled at her own joke for a moment. "I thought I was really, really in love with him for a while, but when the case was over, and I didn't have to stay in character, some of the magic just got lost, and it all got a little... well, boring. I had really been looking forward to just being myself again and being appreciated for who I really am, but I guess somehow my feelings for him were intertwined with the mission, the thrill. Pretending to be someone else. I suppose that in the end, it was my character that fell for him."

Elin took a deep sip from her drink.

"Besides, at the end of the day, he's a criminal and has always been. Our worldviews are just so different. Once the first infatuation wore off, I just kept seeing him as this guy who is not evil or anything but somehow always ends up making wrong life-choices."

"I understand. To be honest, I never quite understood what you saw in him. He didn't seem like a hardened bad guy. I think his heart was in the right place, but still, I think you could afford to be a little pickier."

Gunvor couldn't stop herself, even though she felt like she was talking like a mother.

"I know, Gunvor. David and I have gone over it all on the phone."

Gunvor sat back in her chair and gazed at her young friends. Two months ago, she would not have been able to picture this dinner in her wildest imaginations. When she first met them, they were like cats and dogs. David had been very abusive, and Gunvor had played at high stakes putting the two of them together. In the end, fortunately, her gut feeling had proven to be right. Once they had been removed from their toxic environments, they were getting along perfectly well. It warmed her heart to see that they still seemed fond of each other, even outside the investigation context.

"That's good. Oh, and how is school? Not long until graduation, right?"

"It's been good, I'm a real swot, but it's actually been kind of chill, even with the exams getting closer. We have two or three afternoons off every week to study, but I don't really need all that time. It's been a little bit boring, to be honest. But I guess I should enjoy it while it lasts."

"Do you have any plans for when school is over?"

"I think I'm just going to work for a bit and save up some money to travel. Maybe even apply to some universities abroad. I would just feel a bit bad for leaving mom here alone."

Gunvor noticed the concern in Elin's eyes.

"I can assure you your mother would be overjoyed if you set out to travel. It's only natural for a mother to be a little worried when their young fly the coop. No matter how grown up they are. I know you've told me about your mother's fear of having ruined your life. I can guarantee that fear is worse. If you set out to explore the world, that will be proof for her that you are doing just fine after all."

She patted Elin fondly on her shoulder.

"I guess you're right."

"And you can't just live for your parents. You've got to live your own life."

David had entered the conversation again. The other two nodded in agreement. When he felt he could steer the conversation a little without being rude to Elin, he turned to Gunvor.

"So, what's new with you? Are you working on any new cases?" He said with anticipation in his voice.

"Yes, actually, now that you mention it. I just saw a new client at the office this morning. A woman whose husband has gone missing. If you ask me, I'd say he's left of his own free will, but either way, I'm tasked with finding him."

"Anything we can help with?"

"Not at the moment. But I promise, if anything comes up, I'll let you know. There's just not a lot to go on at this stage. He put in for a two-week leave of absence at his work without telling the wife. So, my guess is that he's with a mistress somewhere and will turn up on his own accord sooner or later, and at that point, at least one of them will file for divorce."

"So, what's your plan until he does?" Elin had also taken an interest in the case.

"I'll go and check their vacation home in the archipelago tomorrow."

"Check for what?"

"For him, he might very well be there. The wife has just assumed that he's not because he's not picking up on the landline. If he is not there, there might be some clues as to where he's gone. She won't let me in their home, so this is pretty much my only prospect."

" Okay, well, you know where to find us if you need any help."

"I do, and I'm grateful for it." Gunvor would happily put her young friends on the case even if it meant paying them out of her own pocket. Not that the turnover for her services was much to brag about, but the savings account from her time at the hospital was still more or less untouched. As a matter of fact, it had grown quite substantially when the house got sold in the divorce, and she moved into the rental. But it didn't make much sense bringing two extra people along just to have a look around an old house.

The evening went on in high spirits until long after midnight. It was well past Gunvor's usual bedtime, and finally, she had to excuse herself. When she had closed the door behind Elin and David, she could still hear them in the stairwell, arguing about which nightclub to go to that night.

CHAPTER 10
SATURDAY, OCTOBER 31

GUNVOR GOT herself a cup of coffee and a Swedish meatball sandwich from the small onboard ferry café. She had unsuccessfully tried masking the beverage's sour tang with excessive amounts of milk, and now it caused her to make an involuntary grimace. She took the first bite of the sandwich as the boat left the quayside and turned around; it gave her a good view of the inlet in the late autumn sun. She smiled to herself. It had been years since she last visited the archipelago. It was gorgeous at this time of the year, with all its red and yellow leaves. The Cedergren's house was situated between two ferry stops, Sand and Solvik. She had decided to get off at Solvik on her way there and then take the ferry from Sand on her way back home. That way, she would get an overview of the surrounding area.

The ride to Nämdö would take at least a couple of hours. She picked up her notebook to write down any thoughts that came to mind as the little ferry shuffled its way across the water among the islands and skerries. The weather was cool, but she had dressed for the occasion. Boots lined with wool, denim jeans, and an old down jacket. Not very fashionable, but functional and comfortable now that the temperature had dropped almost to the freezing point. The coat was a relic from her years with Rune. It had been bought sometime in the early days before they had lost each other in that big house. Back when they still used to take all those long walks together, no matter the season, in all types of weather. It had been a brief but happy time, followed, of course, by years of gloom and boredom. Years that blended into each other and devoured the weeks and months and turned them all into a thick grey soup.

People flooded out of the ferry as soon as they docked at Solvik. When Gunvor stepped onto land, she spotted a supermarket with a sign that said Anne's Groceries and a restaurant. The area reserved for outdoor seatings had been emptied out for the season, but inside the red wooden building, the lunch service was in full swing. It seemed like a nice enough restaurant, but Gunvor was still full from the sandwich and decided to get mineral water at Anne's Groceries instead. And while she was in there, perhaps she could manage to extract some useful information from the cashier. The woman behind the counter looked confused at first when Gunvor mentioned the names Eva and Per Cedergren but nodded once she described the location of their house.

"I don't see them around too much. They're not in here a lot. I think they probably get off the ferry at Sand usually, which is a little closer to their house. They have their own boat as well, don't they? I know they have a landing stage, at least. I used to know the couple that owned that house before them. It's very nice. They have their own little cove almost, so you get some privacy, unlike many of the lots on the island."

This was interesting news to Gunvor. Eva had not mentioned a boat.

"We keep tabs on each other here, you know," the cashier said with a wink. "Why are you asking, anyway?"

The question was very straightforward, and Gunvor could not come up with a way of deflecting it without seeming suspicious. Eva had not, technically, asked her to keep quiet about the investigation, so she decided to tell the cashier the truth.

"The husband has been reported missing. I'm a private investigator."

The cashier gasped in surprise and, Gunvor assumed, to some degree, excitement. She hoped that, since she had disclosed what she was doing there, maybe the cashier would be willing to spill a little extra gossip and hopefully give away some useful information.

"Do you know anything about them?"

"I can't say that I do. They are always very fit and well dressed. I guess they put a lot of effort into appearance. They've always been friendly and polite when they've been in here. Especially the husband. She seems a bit more reserved."

She paused and scratched her head.

"Come to think of it I haven't seen them here together in a long time. She seems to be doing most of the shopping. I guess he's busy at work and leaves the rest up to her." She gave a short laugh. "That's how it goes in our generation, I suppose."

The woman behind the counter looked like she was about fifty years old. Even though that meant there was a gap of a good ten years between the two of them, it seemed true enough that they would both be children of the same outdated gender mentality.

As more people came into the store, Gunvor decided that it was best to conclude the conversation. She did not want to stir up too much gossip on the island, although the damage might already have been done.

"Thanks for the information. I should be going."

"That's nothing, have a nice day. The restaurant next door is open until 2 pm if you get hungry."

Outside, the sun was shining again. Gunvor closed her eyes and took a deep breath of the crisp, cold air. The pebblestones scrunched pleasantly under her boots as she walked down the narrow road, squiggling between houses and woodland scenery, parallel to the cute shoreline cottages and their little gardens surrounded by the colorful autumn forest. Just a few weeks from now, all those leaves would be lying on the ground in a decomposing brown mush as the archipelago entered its long and deep winter sleep.

She walked past the white wooden church Eva had described to her, where the forest path to the house led up. A few minutes later, she approached a red gate with a sign, welcoming guests to the Cedergren family house.

It didn't take long for Gunvor to confirm that Eva had been right all along. No-one appeared to have been on the lot recently. The windows of the house were all dark, and the lawn was covered in fallen leaves. She knocked on the front door and waited a moment before entering. Once inside, she noticed that the house did not quite have the feeling of an uninhabited summer house, after all. The air inside felt fresh, a stark contrast to the stale smell that had greeted her in her own hallway just days before. The temperature was warm and pleasant, not what you would expect in an empty house at this time of year. Although, she thought, maybe Eva had put on some extra heating for her, as a friendly gesture. Perhaps they had that type of remote access air conditioner Kjell had been going on about getting for his house.

Gunvor pulled off her boots and began looking around the house. The ground floor consisted of a kitchen, a dining/living room, and a bathroom. The second floor had two bedrooms and a little wardrobe area with a hatch that led up to the attic. One of the bedrooms was furnished with a king-size bed, the other one with a small single bed and a desk. Gunvor noted that the furniture looked exclusive but not very inviting. She wondered quietly whether the single bed was for guests only or if they were sleeping in separate rooms.

The living room had large windows facing the shore, and a glass door led out to a spacious terrace. The walls, ceiling, and floor were all white stained wood and in the far corner stood a whitewashed fireplace. Most of the furniture was also white. A cream sofa with matching cushions had angels embroidered on them. Bookshelves and pedestals ran along the walls, and an old turntable sat on one of the pedestals. Gunvor discovered the landline telephone that Eva had mentioned. She grabbed the phone off its hook and held it to her ear. She thought maybe it had somehow been disconnected, but the dial tone was loud and clear. She dialed her own phone number just to be sure, and after a few seconds, the phone started buzzing in her jacket.

The only thing that broke up all the white was a black TV and a framed black and white photograph hanging above it. It looked like it was taken in the '50s or '60s. Two young men were in white shirts, with rolled-up sleeves and tucked in wide-cut dress pants, laying in the grass. Closely together. One of them, looking into the camera with hazy eyes, looking without seeing, his mind someplace else—perhaps on the other man's hand, which rested on his arm.

Gunvor got caught in the photo for a moment. It had a delicate sensuality to it. A barely noticeable intimacy. But not enough to give life to the sterile living room. All in all, it reminded her more of a hospital room than a vacation home.

The kitchen was white too. Small and without any seating. Two countertops stood facing each other with accompanying shelves in the middle of the room, and a neat pantry, with vintage style jars and tins in perfect rows. Gunvor was a little surprised to find the refrigerator plugged in. However, there was nothing in there that could give her any clues as to whether anyone had stayed in the house recently—just three bottles of Chablis and a jar of Kalamata olives.

Next to one of the countertops stood a wine rack that was almost high enough to reach the ceiling. Gunvor looked closer at a few bottles, mostly driven by her curiosity and interest in wine. When she realized that the rack contained not only red wine, which had been her assumption, but also white wine and champagne, something tingled inside her. That meant that they did not just stash all their white wine in the refrigerator. Someone wanted these three bottles cooled for a purpose. Granted, it could be that the couple just kept a few bottles in there to make sure they had something to drink if they ever came out here straight from work on a Friday evening. But it could also mean that Per was actually around. Her pulse raced. She instinctively looked out the window, but the garden was as solitary and quiet as before.

She left the glass door open behind her as she stepped out on the terrace. She did not bother tying her shoelaces. Just tucked them in the boots. Four wooden steps brought her down on the lawn. At the far end stood a small shed, from where the narrow path down to the private wooden dock began. Gunvor could make out a large boat down there. She had never taken an interest in boats, so she could not tell too much about it, other than it was one of those large motorboats people would cook and sleep and spend their entire vacations on. She had a hard time picturing Eva doing that, though. Not that she knew her at all, and she did look fit and well-exercised to handle it without any effort. But she could not shake the prejudice that life on a boat would be too cramped and uncomfortable for her taste.

The scent of firewood from the shed was pleasant but also aroused some melancholy in Gunvor. As her fingers slid across the chopping block, she was drawn into a memory from her first year with Rune. Before they moved to Saltsjöbaden and the great house. It was a memory from their very first summer vacation. They had rented a small cottage on the west coast. Even though it had been a hot summer, it had become almost like a ritual to fire up the sauna down by the little wooden dock every night. They had taken turns chopping the wood. Rune had insisted on doing it himself, but Gunvor would not hear it. Despite her small stature, her arms had always been strong. Besides, chopping wood was, like most things in this world—all technique.

Her fingers lingered on a deep groove in the chopping block. For some reason, they had always tried to place the ax into the same spot of the block, with one last swing, once they had enough wood. It seemed like whoever did the chopping around here had the same habit. Although there was no ax to be seen, she peeked into the shed but saw nothing but wood. It was probably locked in the house somewhere, safety first.

She walked down to the boat and jumped aboard, shouting *hello*, without expecting anyone to answer. The boat was as abandoned as the house. The cashier had been on point with her description of the surroundings. The dock was indeed very isolated. Standing here, it was hard to believe that the closest neighbor was just a few minutes away.

Once back at the house, she sat down on the terrace for a while. The cell phone signal was pretty bad out there, just as

Eva had said, but she managed to call the landline inside the house just to make absolutely sure that the phone worked properly. It immediately started ringing with a loud and annoying tone. Whether Per had been in the house when Eva had called and chosen not to pick up for one reason or another was still anyone's guess. But if he had been there, he would have heard the call.

Gunvor had a hard time getting her head around why Eva had even bothered to hire a private investigator to find Per if she did not suspect that he was cheating on her. He had clearly left on his own account, and judging from the fact that he had requested just a two-week leave from work, it seemed probable that he would show up again before long.

At last, she got up from her seat to do one last search of the house before heading back to the city. She had been at the house long enough that if Per had just been out for a walk, he would have been back by now. There was, of course, the possibility that he had seen her there and had deliberately kept out of sight. He might even have mistaken her for a burglar. Either way, it did not seem like a good use of time and resources to stick around the house for too long.

Just in case he would come back to the house before anyone else heard from him, she left a note on the dining table.

You're missed, and you're making your wife
spend a lot of money on a private investigation.
Just give her a call.

There was a considerable risk that Eva would take issue with the note, should she ever see it. But Gunvor thought to herself that Per Cedergren should know what problems he was causing and, if he saw it, it might just give him a push in the right direction.

Gunvor had already tied her boots back on and was

reaching for the front door when she saw it. A small, yellow piece of paper. Only a single corner of it peeked out from under the doormat. Must have been entirely covered by the mat until just then, when she stepped on it, making it slide a couple of inches across the wooden floor. Otherwise, she should have discovered it when she first entered the house.

She kneeled to pick it up.

Nytorget, Urban Deli.

It was a small flyer about the size of a regular business card, bright yellow with a black logo, and the address and phone number of the restaurant. She flipped it over and found that someone had put down another phone number with blue ink. She left the house with a smile on her lips. Happy that she had acquired at least one possible lead. If nothing else, it was enough to keep her occupied on the ferry back to the city.

CHAPTER 11
SUNDAY, NOVEMBER 1

IT WAS ALMOST afternoon when Aidan finally woke up. He had gotten home late the night before. Very late. Or very early, depending on how you are counting, since it had actually been morning rather than night when he had finally gotten into bed. He reached for his glasses on the nightstand before he made an attempt to sit. A familiar sensation settled like a heavy crown over his forehead, and his mouth reminded him of a dry leather satchel. He had been out every night since Wednesday. Not that he could not hold his liquor. He and Gunvor would regularly share a couple of bottles of wine on a nice evening. And in the summertime, as it were, most evenings could be considered nice. But he was not at all used to being up this late.

Friday and Saturday had been more or less interchangeable. They had been around the clubs Aidan was acquainted with. Their tactic had been simple. Order a drink from the bar, sit down and observe which of the bartenders seems most friendly and talkative with the guest. Aidan would then approach that person, holding up the photo of Seb from

Marie's phone. He would tell them a story about how he had met Seb in that same bar, and they had been getting along so well, but just as things had gotten interesting, Aidan had received an emergency phone call from his work. They had agreed to meet again, and Seb had given Aidan his number, but somehow it had gotten erased from Aidan's phone. At this part of the story, Aidan looked as sad and miserable as he could and told the bartender in a confiding tone that he just could not stop thinking of Seb, and it would be such a waste if he could not at least meet him one more time just to see if maybe they could have something real. He would give anything for a chance of that. Finally, he added that he would be willing to offer a finder's fee to anyone that could help him. Wherever they went, he told that same story.

Aidan felt good about his enactment and the idea of adding the finder's fee. He was confident that if they ever bumped into anyone who actually knew anything, they would try and help him out.

The night before had ended at a club called Wonk. When Aidan had asked the bartenders, they had all, to his disappointment, seemed hesitant and given very similar answers; that it was a large venue with a lot of guests coming and going. That Seb seemed a bit old to be hanging out there and that he at least was not a regular. So, he and Marie planted themselves at the bar to keep a lookout on their own.

It had been crowded and loud, but not unpleasant. The context could have been a bit more lighthearted, of course, than looking for a friend who had mysteriously vanished. But after a couple of drinks, Marie too had seemed quite relaxed. They had even danced. Aidan was not a big dancer, but the music had been good, and on a sudden whim, he had told Marie that they might get an even better overview of the venue from the dance floor. When the DJ played a slow song, he moved in closer. She let him lead her, but her body was stiff. He could not make out if it was because she did not know how to dance either, or if she was uncomfortable with the sudden intimacy. So, he restrained from making any further moves, even though he was slowly admitting to himself that her serious personality attracted him. Her green eyes were among the most beautiful he had ever seen.

He finally mustered up the strength to get out of bed and jumped in for a quick shower. Once dressed, he went down the apartment building stairs to knock on Gunvor's door in the hope of some good coffee. He knew that Gunvor would probably read him like an open book. He was not about to spill his guts about his feelings for Marie. Whatever they were. He was not quite sure himself. He knew that he was attracted to her, but he was not so sure that he wanted to make something more out of it. And he had a hard time deciphering the signals Marie was giving him. Besides, he had been in enough passionate relationships to know how quickly feelings can change. One day you would feel like you could not possibly go on with your life without a person—someone who became your whole world for a short while. And then, all of a sudden, the feelings would fade, and you would end up all alone again, trying to figure out what went wrong. Or sometimes, why you had ever been drawn to the person in the first place.

Another thing to take into consideration was his new role as an investigator. He was excited to have some real say in a case finally. For now, at least, that was more important than how things turned out between him and Marie. He knew that he was not willing to risk being taken off the case because of some display of affection that might not be reciprocated. Given that she was reserved and kept her feelings to herself, he decided that it was impossible for the time being to get a read on her feelings about him. It was probably for the best to just focus on finding Seb—for now.

To Aidan's delight, Gunvor was home and awake. They prepared a breakfast consisting of smoothies with added protein and a light roast Kamwangi PB, brewed in the new coffee maker. While the fragrance of the coffee spread throughout the kitchen, Aidan told Gunvor briefly about the stakeout the previous night, leaving out the slow dance.

"What about your case? Making any progress?"

Gunvor nodded keenly and told him about the trip to the cabin and the note with the phone number. She then took out her phone, entered a number, and activated the speakerphone. The call went straight to voicemail.

"Hello, naughty people. This is Felix, your friendly provider. Let me know what *you* need after the beep, and I will get back to you. Don't forget to leave your name and number."

Gunvor and Aidan looked at each other in silence for a moment.

"Drugs?"

"Right? But isn't it a little too obvious?" Gunvor was not completely convinced, although she could not think of any plausible alternatives.

"I suppose you don't necessarily have to be a genius to get in the business?"

"I wouldn't be so sure. He's not explicitly saying that he's selling drugs, and he does demand a name and number. I assume for vetting customers. And he's using a pay as you go sim-card, so there's no way to trace him just based on that number."

"So, did you leave your name and number?"

"Sure did. I left a voicemail explaining that I'm just looking for a missing person that happened to have his number, and all I'm looking for is a way to find him."

"Good, let's just hope he's a drug dealer with some chivalry. Did you find any other clues?"

Gunvor held up the yellow card with the number and flipped it, showing the logo for Urban Deli.

"I might have. I'm going there now to see what I can find out."

"Oh, nice. Great food."

"Have you been there?" Gunvor got excited.

"Yes, just for lunch, but it's really good. I would go with you, but I have to meet up with Marie." Aidan was a little disappointed in missing out on the prospect of a great lunch and some possibly interesting reconnaissance work.

"Maybe another time then, when you're free. I could always call in the Fruängen Bureau."

CHAPTER 12

REGARDLESS OF THE biting autumn breeze, Gunvor enjoyed her slow walk between the subway station and Nytorget. She had even gotten off the train at Skanstull to indulge in a little nostalgia. Even though she had been drowning in work for most of her life, there had been times when she had been able to let everything go, if only for a few hours. Much of that had been thanks to Lars, her best friend and colleague during her years at the hospital. With an almost superhuman effort, he had convinced her to spend a night out once in a while. These were usually occasions when Rune was away on one of his many business trips to America. She smiled as she walked past the familiar entrance of Pelikan. A lovely, old beer hall where she and Lars had consumed countless pilsners while working through a menu of well-made, rustic traditional Nordic food.

Gunvor and Lars were, in many ways, each other's counterparts. The one thing they really had in common was their curiosity. But despite that, or maybe because of that, they had always enjoyed each other's company and had a lot of fun together. Lars was one of the original punk rockers who, following his rebellious youth, had shown a prodigious talent for psychiatry. Gunvor, on the other hand, had always been a swot—keeping her head in the books—and then, later on, turned into a workaholic of great proportions. Except for a short period in the early '80s, she had spent most of her nights either studying or working. She was still like that in many ways, but Lars had shown her that sometimes, doing everything right and by the book can be a crutch and stop you from reaching your full potential. This was something she had taken to heart and applied to her new career path.

Thinking about it, she was suddenly overcome with a guilty conscience. It had been a long time since she promised to get in touch with him as soon as she started feeling better. After her career came to an abrupt stop — the result of tremors in her hands that had almost cost a patient's life—she had stayed clear of everything and everyone that reminded her of the incident. Her antipathy towards aging and her inability to forgive herself had left her without a choice. When Lars finally, after many unanswered phone calls, texts and emails, had shown up at her doorstep to make sure that she was alright, she assured him that she would get back to him. But she had yet to fulfill that promise.

It was not like she did not miss him. She did. Her friendship with Aidan had filled some of the void that Lars had left, but one friend cannot really replace another. Maybe it was time to see the accident for what it was, finally. In the end, the only thing hurt was her pride and self-esteem. She knew that one day, she would have to let it go.

She crossed over Katarina Bangata to Södermannagatan for another block before taking a right onto Skånegatan. Her melancholy grew even stronger as she slowed down her pace and peeked through the windows of restaurant Chanti. Once, the space had been occupied by a wonderful tiny bar called Levelius. There had only been room for a counter and a couple of tables. But a ledge on one of the walls had been fitted with a piano that anyone who felt so inclined could climb up to and pick out a few tunes. The owner would usually conclude the night by getting up there to perform an aria for the guests, and the bartenders all made an effort trying to remember the names of every customer. The atmosphere had always been warm and chaotic, with a farrago of young artists, stage actors, and old worn-out women and men who spent most of their time and money at the little bar.

Finally, she arrived at Nytorget and walked through the doors of Urban Deli. She had to agree with Aidan—the place did seem lovely. The first thing that greeted her was a delicatessen, filled with oils and pickles of all kinds in beautiful cans and bottles, fresh produce, and a long stretching counter filled with cheeses and charcuterie. Behind all this, in the back of the room, was the restaurant with big glass windows overlooking Nytorget. Gunvor decided on a fish stew and a glass of the house white. It was busy, but by no means overcrowded, so Gunvor easily managed to get a seat where she could see most of the comings and goings in the restaurant and the kitchen. The outdoor beer garden was long closed for the winter season. Gunvor sighed at the thought of the long dark winter waiting to make its big entrance any day now. It was already November, and for a moment, she wished that she had stayed a while longer with Kjell at Gran Canaria.

She intended to discreetly observe the restaurant while having her lunch and then approach a suitable staff member with Per's photo. She wanted to determine who seemed to be most acquainted with the guests, or at least most sociable, and, therefore, most likely to have any valuable information and, perhaps even more important, be willing to share it. It was a Sunday, so if this place had any regulars, this would be the day to show up. A stroll in the city and a visit to a favorite bar were popular ways to conclude the weekend for many people in the city.

The wine was decent, and the food was bordering on exquisite. She had to make an effort to eat slowly and keep her eyes on the surroundings rather than the delicious stew. The atmosphere among the staff appeared to be warm and friendly. They seemed to enjoy each other's company, milling about and chatting to one another whenever they got a chance. Any relationships with the customers were less obvious, and there were no signs of any regulars yet. One of the waiters gave a man an extra warm welcome, but it turned out to be a friend coming to pick him up after work.

Ever since hearing the outgoing voicemail on Felix's phone, she had been pondering what kind of role drugs could possibly have in this case. The most likely explanation would be that Per just wanted to spice up his nights out with whatever drug was popular these days. In the 80s, it had been cocaine for people with money who wanted to stay awake and keep partying. In the posher clubs, it had been more or less in the open. Gunvor herself had never shown any interest and was clueless about what drugs people might have moved on to since then.

There were no signs of drug trading or other illegal activities in the restaurant. Even if Per had met Felix at Urban Deli, it did not necessarily mean any business was conducted here. Not that it really mattered; the drugs were likely irrelevant to the case. The important thing was to find Felix and see if he knew anything about Per's whereabouts. If the two men were friendly, there was a chance Per had told him about his plans.

When one of the waiters passed her table, she made a quick decision.

"Hi, excuse me."

The waiter stopped in his tracks and gave Gunvor a friendly smile.

"How can I be of service?"

It was a man in his fifties. His hair was neatly slicked back with elegant grey streaks, and he was evidently in very good shape for his age, with a slender waistline, a broad torso, and muscular arms bulging under his shirt.

"Do you know a Per Cedergren? I think he comes here a lot."

The waiter answered without any hesitation.

"I know only very few of our customers by name. Although some of them like to chat, people come here because they're interested in the food—and each other."

He smirked as he uttered the last words.

Gunvor assumed that it was more or less an auto-reply, and it made sense. Even if the waiters were not forced to sign confidentiality agreements, it was probably frowned upon to be seen gossiping. She lowered her voice and tried to look as grave as possible.

"I'm a private investigator."

She paused for a second to let that sink in, and when she saw the familiar spark of curiosity light up his eyes, she continued.

"He has gone missing."

With that, she held up a picture of Per. The waiter accepted it and studied it carefully.

"He has likely disappeared on his own accord, but his friends and family are very worried."

"I've seen him around." He stopped for a second to think. "I don't really know anything about him, other than that he more often than not doesn't leave alone—if you know what I mean."

"I see. That has kind of been my suspicion that he has left to be with someone." Gunvor figured she might as well confide in the waiter now that he was being helpful. If he felt involved, he might be more motivated to remember more details. "Do you know if he's been here with someone named Felix? I came across one of your cards with his number written on the back of it at Per's house. I tried calling, but it goes straight to voicemail."

On hearing this, the waiter suddenly looked concerned.

"Well, actually, we do have someone named Felix among the staff. He usually fills in, but we haven't been able to get in touch with him for the past week. I mean, it's probably not the same Felix, but I've been trying to reach him because we've been short-staffed and could really have used his help. It's unlike him not to answer or call back. He normally gets back to us even if it's just to say that he can't take the shift."

"That is a curious coincidence." Gunvor tried to piece together and make sense of the information she had just received. Were the disappearances linked somehow?

"I really hope nothing terrible has happened."

"Oh, I wouldn't worry too much. In the absolute majority of these cases, people turned up unscathed sooner or later with a more or less logical explanation." She smiled encouragingly to the waiter in a way she hoped he would find reassuring.

"Do you know if these two gentlemen know each other?"

He thought about this for a second before shaking his head.

"I think I've seen them talk at some point but, that could totally have been Felix just taking an order. I could ask my colleagues. Are you sticking around for a bit?"

"Absolutely." She handed the waiter her business card even though they would soon talk again. "In case I forget later, if you come to think of anything, anything at all, I would love to hear about it."

The memory of the bartender she had trusted for information in her last case flashed back for a second and sent a chill down her spine. She had naively believed that she was getting help from a staff member at Sturehof, but in the end, he had turned to be an ally of the shadow figure they were after. The mistake did nearly cost her, and more importantly, Elin's life. She quickly tried to calm down by telling herself that this would be nothing like the last case—just a husband cheating on his wife. No-one would get hurt.

"Oh, one last thing before you go. Would you give me the phone number of Felix so that I can see if it matches the one I have?" She cursed herself for almost forgetting something so obvious. She smiled at the waiter, hoping it would seem like she had just waited for the right moment.

"I'll see what I can do."

Gunvor decided to be happy with her effort despite almost forgetting a vital clue. No harm done, so no reason to beat herself up about it.

She did not have to wait long before the waiter returned to the table. None of the other staff members had any information about Felix and Per other than that Felix had been seen serving him on occasion.

"You know I'm not really allowed to do this."

He reached into his apron and returned the photo together with a note with a number scribbled on it.

"Promise that you'll let me know if you hear from him or find out anything. I mean Felix."

"I promise. You too?"

He nodded before taking the few steps back to his station behind the bar. Gunvor compared the numbers. They did not match. Just as she suspected. If it was the same Felix, and he had used that same number for his day job, with that voicemail, he would really have been as stupid as Aidan first thought. She called the new number. After a few signals, there was an outgoing voicemail message. The voice did sound similar to the one in the other message, it could definitely be the same person, but she could not be sure. The real upside was that this number was registered to a Felix Wiik, whereas the other number was untraceable. That meant she would easily be able to find out his home address. If this turned out to be the same Felix, the investigation was now getting traction. Excited, she scrolled through her contacts until she found the number for David.

CHAPTER 13

AIDAN AND MARIE had arranged to meet at The Chocolate Cup in Old Town to discuss how they were going to move forward with the investigation. Aidan had been at the café once before with Drew, who had told him the place was a known gay hotspot. He remembered it as a nice place. They had struck up a lively conversation almost immediately with the party at the neighboring table.

He was going to suggest to Marie that they should try looking for Per at Patricia—an old boat turned into a nightclub down by the docks at Södermälarstrand—after the meeting. They hosted a gay night every Sunday. But before he moved forward, he wanted to make sure Marie was committed, or at least interested, in keeping the search going. She had not mentioned anything about it, secretive as she was, but tomorrow was Monday. Presumably, she had to go to a job of some sort. Aidan had the privilege of being able to push the bulk of his work to the afternoons when he did most of his teaching. But even so, he could not go on sleeping through the mornings for much longer. He would normally spend at least a few hours before lunch preparing lectures and course material. On the other hand, if Marie wanted to go on with the search, he did not want to pass that up. He would have to find a way to make it work.

The café was almost empty, aside from the two of them and two other couples. One of them holding hands and with their heads close together. Aidan felt a little sting of envy of their infatuation.

"I really don't understand how he can lurk around these kinds of places." Marie suddenly hissed.

"What do you mean?"

"You know."

Marie had seemed a little on edge ever since she walked in.

"Gay bars? I suppose our generation has had... are having difficulties accepting gay people. It doesn't make much sense when you think about it. People seem to have this built-in obsession that everyone should be exactly the same. It's not like being gay is hurting or even affecting anyone else. Honestly, I cannot wrap my head around why people are so upset. It's all positive things in a person's life, really. Love, attraction, sex—I don't see how that's anyone else's problem. I, for one, wouldn't appreciate anyone else trying to control who I should have feelings for."

Aidan's attempt at a flirtatious smile while uttering the last sentence either was not registered or had no effect on Marie. She turned her head to look out the window like a sullen child.

"But he's not some faggot!"

The sudden outburst of rage threw Aidan off to the degree that he stumbled on his words when he replied.

"Woah, excuse me? What the hell? What does that even mean? Is he not gay all of a sudden? Explain to me then why we've been spending a week looking for him in every gay-club in the city?"

"I guess he has his needs..."

"Needs?"

"Yes."

Marie looked up at him with the face of a defiant teenager. Aidan thought that seemed like a good match for her level argumentation.

"Generally speaking, those kinds of needs are a pretty strong indication of someone being gay, wouldn't you say?

"But I know he's not a fag. We've been together. I mean, we used to be a couple."

"Oh my god, really? Again with the f..."

Aidan froze for a second. Had this investigation just been all about jealousy?

"Hold on, when was this? Why haven't you mentioned this before?"

"Oh, it was a long time ago. High school. Doesn't matter now."

"Then you became friends, just like that?"

Marie nodded.

"And neither of you had any problems with that?"

"Nope."

Aidan studied Marie's face in an attempt to determine whether her short answers did, in fact, mean just the opposite. She did not have him convinced. Although, if they had been together in high school, that was a very long time ago. It would be weird if she were friends with him all these years without letting her feelings go. Right? She must have had lots of relationships since then. But then again, she did seem a little peculiar, especially now. Either way, he decided to keep an open mind to all possibilities. And it did certainly seem like a possibility that she was really more jealous than worried.

"We've always loved each other. But we've never had a passionate relationship. Sex doesn't interest me. It kind of just transformed into a friendship without us really noticing it happening."

Her eyes were fixated on Aidan. Their intensity, in combination with what she had just said, almost made him blush. He could not tell if it had just been a disclosure for their investigation or if she was aware of his feelings towards her. Maybe she wanted to explain herself. He let go of his agitation.

"Hasn't it been painful to love someone for all these years and still not really be together? For me, sex is, above anything else, about intimacy. Closeness to the one you love. Not that it's any of my business, but did anything happen in the past to make you want to keep your distance? Or could it be that maybe you haven't met the right person?

Marie still had her eyes on Aidan, but it was impossible to read her face. She did not look angry, nor cold, but definitely closed off. A look of passive rejection and secrecy. At that moment, Aidan wondered why he had found her so attractive. Her eyes were beautiful, sure. But he did not think of himself as that vain. There was an attraction, no doubt, but he could not quite grasp what was causing it.

"It has nothing to do with that. And this investigation is not about me."

Reluctantly, Aidan accepted that the discussion on that topic was now over.

"So, what do you want to do now? Patricia is open tonight. It could be worth a try. Or do you need to be up for work early tomorrow?

He hoped that his innocent question would generate an answer, giving him a little more insight into her life.

"Let's go."

Marie gulped the last of her coffee in one go and got up to get her coat.

CHAPTER 14

DAVID HAD STUDIED the picture of Per meticulously on the subway ride into the city. It was not a face that was easy to remember. It looked just like any middle-aged man, he thought. Fortunately, it seemed to be a quiet night at Urban Deli. He could easily take his time to have a good look at each and every one of the other guests and compare them to the photo. To his disappointment, there was no match.

He had just ordered his second beer when a man in his mid-sixties sat down on the barstool next to his. David gave the man a slight nod, which the man returned with what David considered an oily smile and a wink. After making his order at the bar, he turned back to David with a flirtatious smile and a breath that reeked of wine.

"What's a little kitten like you doing out all by yourself on a Sunday night, then?

"Eh... I'm just having a beer." David had no interest in making conversation but felt like he should at least be polite.

The scrawny man just kept staring at him with watery eyes. David, in turn, tried to lean back to avoid his breath.

"Yes, I can see that. Cheers!" The man raised the glass the bartender had just put in front of him.

David saw no other option than to raise his glass, with a light nod, and take a sip. He then pretended to text on his phone, but he could still feel the man's gaze as if it was burning on his skin.

"I haven't seen you around. Are you new to the game?" The man leaned in close enough that David could feel the wind of his breath on his cheek.

"What fucking game, man?

The sudden aggression in David's voice made the man jump back a little, but the second after, he seemed to have forgotten about it. Suddenly his hand was on David's thigh.

"I think you know what game. I might look old. But these years come with experience. If you need someone to bareback, you just say the word."

"Hey, hey, leave the kid alone." One of the bartenders came up between them. David had been just a millisecond from losing his temper and shoving the old man away. The bartender had apparently picked up on this. Or maybe this was not the first time the old man had been harassing other guests. The bartender's voice was gentle but firm.

"Why don't you go and take a seat with Sven. He's used to your shenanigans." He pointed to an older gentleman across the bar and gave the man a light push in Sven's direction.

"I'm sorry. He's harmless, but he can be a nuisance when he's had too much. He's getting old and pathetic. Just like me." He gave David a gloomy smile.

"It's fine," David attempted to smile back even though he felt anything but fine. How the hell could that old man think he would be interested in doing anything with him. What a pervert. David did not know what barebacking meant, but whatever it was, he felt sure he would not appreciate doing it with the old man. He took a deep breath and did his best to let go of the incident.

As the night went on, more and more people started filling up the restaurant. The atmosphere, however, never got very rowdy. The guests were mostly couples or groups of friends having dinner. A few others sat by the bar, alone. But most of them seemed quiet and to themselves, unlike David's new acquaintance. It occurred to David that the people at the bar were all men. He tried to figure out if that was unusual or not. Did women ever sit alone in bars? It often happened in films, but he could not remember ever seeing that happen in real life. Maybe that's why Gunvor had called him first and not Elin.

CHAPTER 15

GUNVOR WAS IN LUCK. She had just confirmed that the gate leading into the stairway of Anders Reimers Street 14 was locked, just like she thought it would be, when a man walking a small dog came strolling towards the building. When Gunvor realized that he was deep in his own thoughts, she picked up her phone and pretended to be on a call.

"I'm just outside your building now. Could you come down and let me in? Oh, wait, there's someone going in now. Maybe he'll let me in. Hold on...."

Gunvor turned to the man who was just fiddling with his keys and gave him her most charming smile.

"Would it be alright if I snuck in with you, so my son won't have to come down and get me?"

She held her breath, hoping the man didn't know Felix well enough to realize that she was not his mom. But he did not even ask who she was visiting.

"Of course." The man smiled back and held up the door for her.

Gunvor glanced as discreetly as she could at the plaque by

the entrance, listing all of the residents of the building. She found the name Wiik, listed on the ground floor. The man who had let her in was already halfway upstairs.

"Thank you so much!"

He turned around and waved before disappearing up to the next floor. She found the right door and rang the bell. She could hear the signal buzzing clearly from inside the apartment, but no other sounds. After pushing the button a second time, without a response, she tried to look through the mail drop discreetly. The hallway was dark. A few commercial letters and flyers lay on the floor. On her own door, she had put up a polite but surprisingly effective sign asking the postmen not to deliver any flyers or other advertisements. She could not assess whether these had been from a single delivery or stacked up over time.

She thought about trying one of the neighbors but refrained. What would she say? There was no way she could start asking questions without explaining who she was, and if she did say who she was, that would certainly raise questions. She could not tell his neighbors about the drug suspicions because they were just that, suspicions. And she would not be able to lie and tell them she was a friend or relative because she did not know anything about him.

She decided to head back home, frustrated to leave without any new clues. And worse, the ones she had she could not fit together. To add insult to injury, Aidan was once again busy and would not be able to help her make sense of it all, something to which she had grown accustomed.

CHAPTER 16

THE CONTRAST between the calm atmosphere in the café and the impetuosity of Patricia was shocking. Marie, who had stormed out from the café with such conviction, had slowed down once they were outside. They strolled down past the subway station of Old Town and across the Central Bridge to the quays of Södermälarstrand. The city lights reflected in the calm water and reminded Aidan that his new hometown could be quite stunning in the right conditions.

It could have been a nice moment, but Aidan had not gotten over what had been said in the café, and Marie seemed lost in thought. He wondered what she was thinking about, and if the silence was just another way to distance herself further from him. The night suddenly seemed very gloomy. As if she had heard the thoughts swirling around in his head, Marie stopped abruptly and looked at him.

"I'm really grateful for all your help, you know."

Aidan nodded in silence.

"I know, I'm not always the easiest person to be around." She let her gaze wander from Aidan and out over the dark water. "I guess I'm a classic lone wolf. I don't keep many people around me. Just a few friends that really know me and accept me for who I am. That makes for a very hard blow when someone disappears like this. It's not easy for me to let in new people. As I'm sure you've noticed."

She gave Aidan a shy look before she continued.

"And I guess I'm not very good at expressing my feelings. But I need you to know how much your help means to me, in so many ways. I've never met anyone like you. Someone who's willing to give so much even though we hardly know each other."

At this point, Marie's voice was trembling, and tears started running down her cheeks. Aidan put a tender hand on her shoulder. He could feel her tense up, like a scared animal. But she didn't pull away.

"I'm so sorry—I would really like to. But I just can't. It's too complicated—I hope you understand…"

Aidan did not understand what it was that was so complicated. But he knew people had such different experiences in life and that everyone had their own baggage. So much so that sometimes you cannot understand; you just have to accept. Because Marie was such a reserved person, and he had not known her for very long, it felt futile even to try to imagine what was going on in her head. He considered himself a pretty private person, but it was nothing compared to her.

"If things had been different, I would have loved to. I mean, you seem like such a wonderful person."

"It's okay. Don't worry about it."

He pulled her in for a gentle hug. They remained standing like that. She, with her head resting on his chest. He, with his arms around her. When she finally pulled away, the moment was over. They did not speak of it again.

Despite being pretty worn out from all the previous nights, they decided to have a drink. Aidan looked out over the dance floor as he took his first swigs of the beer. Suddenly, he saw someone out there who looked familiar—a man standing on the far side of the dance floor. For a moment, their eyes locked. The next second, the man leaned forward and whispered something to another man, after which they both pushed through the dance floor and out of the room. Aidan tried to remember why the man seemed so familiar. Was it someone he had shown Seb's photo? Or had he just seen him before in the crowd of one of the clubs?

"Did you see those two guys who just left?"

Marie nodded slowly.

"I spoke to him before I met you that first night."

It all came back to Aidan. He had seen the man when he was waiting for Drew to come back from the dancefloor. He had wondered whether the man was in the same situation as he was because he had also been sitting alone, looking bored.

"Oh, right! If you give me your phone, I'll go talk to him and show him the picture."

"But I just told you I've already talked to him, remember? He'll never buy into your little love-story now."

Aidan nodded but was not quite able to let it go. It was something about that man, the way he had looked at them. Maybe he just recognized them in the same way they recognized him. But perhaps he knew something about Seb, despite not having admitted it to Marie that first time. They were obviously hanging out in the same places. Aidan decided that he needed to investigate further.

"Would you hold on to my beer for a second? I need to go…" He let the last part of the sentence fade out. That way, he could not, technically, be accused of lying. Technically.

Aidan saw the man as soon as he stepped out on the deck. He was leaning against the gunwale, talking in a hushed voice with the man he had just left the dance floor with. When they saw Aidan approaching, the other man strolled off as if it had already been planned.

"Hi there. Sorry to bother you. May I ask you a quick question?"

"Sure. I think I already know what this is about, but let's hear your quick question."

Aidan wasn't sure if the man was polite or mocking, but he went ahead anyway.

"I'm looking for a missing person. Do you know anyone named Seb?"

The man watched Aidan quietly for a while. At last, he nodded slowly.

"Seb is a dear friend of mine."

Aidan felt a rush of adrenaline running through his body. Finally. Progress.

"Do you know where he is?"

The man seemed to weigh his words carefully. There was no longer any doubt that he knew something. It was a matter of how much Aidan could get him to tell.

"I do. He is fine. There is something he has to do. And she can't know about it. Not yet."

Aidan was thrown. She? Marie? What couldn't she know, and why? The man spoke again.

"I haven't told you anything. You've never even seen me. Get it?"

With those words, Aidan was left alone on the deck. He was relieved that Seb was okay but had no idea what to tell Marie.

When he got back to the bar, she was busy talking to one

of the other guests. She gave Aidan a quick recap of the conversation. The man she was talking to introduced himself as Paul. He knew Seb because he had previously had a fling with one of Paul's best friends. He pointed out the friend on the dance floor and waved to get his attention, but the friend was too consumed with dancing to notice. It was a young man, probably only about half Seb's age.

"Hey, Alex!"

No reaction. Paul sighed and went on to tell the story himself of how Seb had been courting his friend. At first, Alexander had rejected him because of his age. But Seb's persistence had given results, and in the end, they had engaged in an intense, although short, affair. Paul cheerfully told Aidan and Marie about how the couple used to have sex all the time right there in the bathroom stalls at Patricia's. After a while, Alexander had grown tired of the fact that the relationship had been solely on Seb's terms, and they had parted ways. All this had happened about a year earlier, with a few relapses, as Paul put it. It had been a while since he last ran into Seb, but he was not sure if it was weeks or months.

Aidan was still thinking about the conversation up on the deck. He saw the man again on the dance floor, but he showed no signs of recognition. Aidan felt like he should do something, but what? When Marie excused herself to go to the bathroom, he held up his phone and smiled towards it like he was taking a selfie.

They stayed at Patricia for a couple of hours more but could not collect any useful information. Aidan contemplated telling Marie about his meeting on the deck. After all, the reason he was there in the first place was to help her find Seb. It did not make much sense, withholding information from her. But for some reason, he felt reluctant going against the mysterious man. If the man had been speaking the truth, Seb had a reason for his disappearance and specifically did not want Marie to find out where he was or what he was doing. In that case, Aidan did not think it was his place to get in the middle of that. He might ruin something. Even though it was hard to see Marie struggle like this, she would find out that everything was fine soon enough, according to the mysterious man. In the meantime, Aidan would help her keep her spirits up and hopefully get to know her a little better.

They parted for the night outside Patricia. Marie insisted on taking a taxi, despite Aidan's offer to walk her home. He was a little bothered by the fact that he did not even know what part of the city she lived in after spending so much time together. But she was adamant, so there was nothing else for him to do than to shrug it off and start walking towards the subway station at Mariatorget.

When he glanced back at Patricia once more before taking off, something caught his eye. A faint flickering was coming from the top deck. The light of a cigarette. Aidan thought he could just barely make out the silhouette of the mysterious man. But he was not sure. It could just be someone needing a break from the steaming dance floor.

CHAPTER 17

ALEXANDER'S NIGHT had been great. Sure, there had been minor embarrassment when the two men he had flirted with had found out about each other, which had subsequently led to him now walking home on his own. He giggled, thinking about it. His plan had been to double his chances. But you cannot win them all. He was not bothered about it, except it would have been nice to have some company walking back home along the dark and empty streets.

Paul had left hours earlier. He had to get up early for work. Still, Alexander was happy that Paul had come out with him for a bit. Although he was a little concerned that he had not really enjoyed himself. He had been sober, in stark contrast to Alexander. That was not normally a problem, but he had looked a little worn out this night. Especially when he had gotten stuck talking to that boring straight old couple, who had apparently been hounding him with questions about Seb. He had seen Paul trying to wave him in from the dance floor to come over to them but pretended not to notice. It would have been such a buzz kill. He felt a little guilty about it now.

Alexander was not a big fan of wandering around alone in the middle of the night. He had always been a little bit scared of the dark, even though he was not quick to admit it. There were still people gathered around outside Patricia, he was hoping that some of them would be going in his direction and for a moment, he thought about asking someone, but decided to look for a taxi instead. The street was empty, so he started walking along the quay towards Hornstull. It was a little annoying that his phone was dead, so he could not just order an Uber. But it was only a matter of time before a free taxi would pass by on the street.

Outside the München Brewery, a gang of drunk men were brawling. Alexander quickened his pace and cursed his fear. Afraid of the dark. Afraid of being jumped by a gang of drunk men who did not like homosexuals. But they did not even seem to take notice of him as he walked past them. They were busy arguing about who should host an afterparty.

Even though the men had not even given him a dirty look, their rowdiness had made Alexander tense. He felt paranoid walking down the street as it got quieter and quieter. A familiar anxiety taking a firm grip of his gut. His own footsteps seemed absurdly loud in the silent night. Where were all the taxis? Why could he not just get over his silly fear of the dark? At home, he always kept at least one light on during the night to feel safe. Out here, the streetlights only seem to make him more exposed and anyone or anything hiding in the shadows even harder to detect. He wished he could use the shadows for cover. Maybe he could leap between the groves and the boats and occasional container? No, that would be insane.

Suddenly, he halted abruptly in his tracks and looked back over the pathway behind him. Was it just his imagination, or had he heard footsteps? His mind could sometimes play tricks on him when he was like this. He stood there for a moment, looking back the way he had come from. Not a soul in sight, the night was quiet. He took a deep breath and closed his eyes for a second to calm his nerves. When he opened them again, there was a dark figure behind one of the parked cars. He blinked his eyes in disbelief. Impossible. Suddenly, the figure leaped towards him. He knew he had to run or scream or fight or do something, but he had lost all control over his body. As the figure approached, something glimmered under the streetlights. The first strike he took to his head. Blinding pain. It only took a light shove to send him over the quayside. By the time his body hit the cold water, he had already long disappeared into the abyss.

CHAPTER 18

MONDAY, NOVEMBER 2

GUNVOR WAS AT A LOSS. The only move forward with the investigation she could think of was to continue the stakeout at Urban Deli. There had to be something else she could do. The waiter had told her that he would let her know if there was any sign of Felix or Per. But he was not always working. Besides, how could she know if he was trustworthy? Gunvor decided to ask Elin to take a shift staking out the restaurant. She would probably want to be part of the investigation, especially now that David was already involved. The big challenge was now to come up with something for herself to do.

She could not help but feel bad charging a desperate wife when it was so obvious that her husband was just out on some adventure. Maybe she should make another attempt at convincing Eva to let her have a look around the couple's home. Or at least Per's study. Or at the very, very least his computer. She felt certain she would find something useful there.

It did not take many seconds for Eva to pick up the phone.

Gunvor took her time carefully explaining the importance of her request to move the investigation forward. Getting access to Per's personal computer could potentially solve the whole case. The likelihood of finding vital information on there was very high. But Eva was not interested. She assured Gunvor that she had already looked through the computer herself, and there was nothing of interest on it.

"Well, to be honest. At this point, there is very little else to go on." Gunvor tried. "Is there anything else that has come to mind since the last time we spoke?"

"No." The answer came immediately.

"And there have been no signs at all of a potential—other woman?" Gunvor felt uncomfortable asking the question so directly, given that Eva had been very clear that she did not buy into that theory. But since Per's father had been so sure of it, and frankly, that was the only explanation for Per's disappearance that seemed plausible to Gunvor, she felt like she had to persist. There could be signs and clues that Eva had failed to process. Clearly, her confirmation bias was against Per being unfaithful.

"Anyone at work he's been working closely with lately, or friends he has spent more time with than usual?"

"There is no other woman. I should know. It's my husband we're talking about here!" At this point, Eva was clearly agitated, and her voice was shrill and piercing.

"I really don't mean to upset you. The thing is, I wouldn't be doing my job very well if I didn't consider the possibility that your husband might be having an affair. It's by far the most common reason for people to disappear like this. Just consider the fact that he did inform his office that he was going to be away for two weeks, but he didn't mention anything to you."

Gunvor felt terrible pushing Eva like this, but it seemed to be the only way forward.

"Maybe he just couldn't take it any longer. I think you should ask Per's father about the way he treats his son."

"I have spoken to Carl. He seemed quite sure that Per is seeing someone and hinted that it's not the first time Per has gotten in trouble, as he put it." Gunvor held her breath after saying this, wondering if she had finally crossed the line.

"Oh, did he now. Of course, he would say that. Carl is the one that gets in trouble. That old man can't keep his hands to himself. It's just wishful thinking from him that Per would be the same. A real old fashion man's man. Per is not like that. He is sensitive and easily manipulated, and Carl runs that company with an iron fist. He's been close to breaking Per completely, many times."

"So, you think he's taking out a vacation to get away for his father for a bit? That doesn't explain why you haven't heard from him. Has this ever happened before?"

"No."

The line went quiet. Gunvor did not know what else to say, so she waited for Eva to either continue or hang up on her.

"When he's in the early stages of a depression, he's good at hiding it. Eventually, he usually opens up. If I just give him a little space, he comes to me when he's ready. Then we can ride it out together. He was always under a lot of pressure and a lot of scrutiny growing up. As an adult, he has had a hard time shaking the habit of always hiding away his feelings. That's what really worries me, more than anything. If he cannot vent his feelings, he might start spiraling into a deep depression. I was already worried when he disappeared. He had been keeping to himself for a while, just burying himself in work, and it didn't seem to get any better...."

Eva's voice was now calm and steady again. Gunvor was a bit torn about her theory but decided to keep her doubts to herself.

"Maybe you should call the police and make a report after all if you're worried about his health. And it might be a good idea to check in with the local hospitals to make sure he hasn't ended up there."

She heard Eva sigh at the other end of the line. It was hard to tell if it was from worry or impatience.

"He's not going to hurt himself. But I need to find him. I want him to know that I'm there for him. Maybe it was a bad idea to hire you. I understand if you don't want to keep going with the investigation."

"I don't mind going on with the investigation. It's just a little hard to know where to look for leads at the moment. But I'll keep pushing." Gunvor did her best to sound convincing even though she had absolutely no idea what to do next.

"Thank you. We'll talk later."

With that, the conversation was over. Gunvor let out a deep sight before picking up the phone again, this time to call Elin.

CHAPTER 19

THERE WERE ONLY a few other guests in the restaurant when Elin walked up to the bar at Urban Deli. It felt odd to order alcohol on an early Monday afternoon. Odd and yet, liberating. During the course of the summer and their last investigation, she had discovered new sides of herself. Some of which she thought were good. Courage and beauty. Others that she was less sure about, like her newfound attraction to alcohol. The latter had gotten more prominent during her short-lived relationship with Chibbe. The fact that he had encouraged that side of her was one reason she had broken up with him. She had left that part out talking to David and Gunvor.

The beer was good. She was more of a wine-person really, but the alcohol percentage in wine seemed a little overboard for the situation.

Gunvor had called in the middle of class. Elin excused herself to the teacher with a gesture signaling that she had to go to the bathroom and picked up the call out in the corridor. It was a call she had longed for, even with their last case having such a dramatic outcome. She had immediately accepted the mission and remained standing in the corridor for a few minutes studying the picture Gunvor had sent her of the missing person before reluctantly going back into class. It was futile trying to keep her focus during the rest of the lecture on the literary esthetics of naturalism.

Elin went to Urban Deli straight from school. They had self-study all afternoon on Mondays. She usually spent the time in the library with some of her classmates, but she had left after lunch, given the particular circumstances. The school lunch was not much to write home about, but it was better than drinking on an empty stomach, so she had forced down some chili con carne and bread.

A man across the bar raised his glass to her in a salute. He gave her a brief smile and took a few sips of his drink before returning to reading his paper. Elin raised her glass as well, relieved that it seemed to have been nothing more than a gesture of courtesy.

At a table by the windows, two elderly ladies shared a late lunch and a glass of white wine. Walking sticks leaned against the wall. Elin thought it seemed wonderful, being a pensioner and just doing whatever you felt like doing. Go for a long walk with your best friend and have wine for lunch. If you could afford it, of course, and were lucky enough to have your health still.

Her eyes wandered across the room as she tried to assess the clientele. Next to the two ladies, three men in their thirties were having a conversation—each with a flat white coffee in front of them. At the table closest to the store sat a lonely man, probably around Gunvor's age, with an almost empty beer. He was looking out the window, seemingly deep in thought. He was tanned, and his light hair must have been dyed. It lacked the grey streaks that would be expected for a man of his age. He was dressed very well but casually. She recognized his scarf from Filippa K, she had wanted to buy the same one for herself, but it had been too expensive.

There were two men sitting by the bar, other than the one that had saluted her. They were seated closely together, one with his hand on the other man's thigh, and seemed to have an intimate conversation.

She looked at the man with the scarf again. Just as she did, he seemed to wake up from his thoughts, and their eyes met for a short second. Elin gave him a little smile and continued to look around the restaurant casually. She did not want him to think that she had been studying him. Out of the corner of her eye, she saw him down the last sip of his beer and get up. A moment later, he stood beside her at the bar, trying to get the bartender's attention.

"Such a nice and calm afternoon." The man said with a friendly smile.

"Yes, it's not every day you get to have a beer at this time of the day."

"Isn't that the truth. Can I offer you a refill? And maybe a little company?"

"That would be lovely, thank you." Elin was genuinely happy about the company. It would have felt weird sitting alone in a bar for hours on end just staring at people. She was sure people would start noticing.

"This is a pretty nice place. I've actually never been here before." Elin did her best to strike up a conversation. The bartender put down the two beers in front of them. The familiar and welcome feeling of intoxication was already slowly creeping up on her.

The man looked her up and down with an amused smile.

"Well, I don't suppose you've been of age for very long, but believe me, you're one lucky goose to have it all in front of you. Unlike a pathetic old bachelor like me." He sighed.

"I don't know if it's really that great to be young. Everyone has all these expectations that you're supposed to make something out of yourself and preferably make the world a better place."

"I'm sorry to be the one to tell you, but that doesn't go away with age. Cheers."

They both raised their glasses.

"I'm Thomas." He offered a firm handshake.

"Elin."

"So, tell me, Elin. What are you really doing here? A young person like yourself could surely find a more suitable place for an afternoon drink. The food is great here and all, but you're not eating, so I'm guessing that's not it. Don't get me wrong; you're just not the typical patron here."

"Well…" Elin was not quite sure how much she was allowed to say about the case and thought about coming up with some kind of story but quickly realized that would be ridiculous. So, she grabbed her phone and found the picture of Per Cedergren.

"This man has disappeared, and I'm trying to help look for him. Do you recognize him?"

Thomas' facial expression when he saw the photo clearly revealed that he did, and as he looked back up at Elin, he nodded.

"I don't know him. But I have seen him around."

Elin felt her pulse rise with excitement. If she could deliver a piece of this puzzle to Gunvor on her very first day, that would be huge.

"Have you ever talked to him?"

"I haven't. And if I ever got the chance, talking wouldn't be the first thing that would come to mind."

Elin stared blankly at him. Thomas cleared his throat before continuing.

"You know, men my age, that know what they want. We don't waste our time with nonsense. And I'm not interested in small talk. I mean, I am with you here, but..." He looked embarrassed when he realized he had entangled himself in his reasoning. "Ah, you know what I mean! With a man like that, you want something else."

It took a few seconds for Elin to understand.

"Oh. But... is he gay?"

Thomas laughed at her puzzled face.

"I couldn't tell you. Most of us regulars are. But then again, as I've said, the food here is great and a lot of people come here for that, and of course everyone is welcome. I don't know what his deal is. I haven't seen anything that points to one thing or another. To be honest, I haven't really paid much attention to him." His face suddenly got serious.

"You're saying he has disappeared, and I'm sitting here making jokes. I'm just awful, aren't I? Do you think something terrible has happened to him?"

"We don't know much, but so far, everything points to him being away by his own free will. Maybe he's met someone and just ditched his wife without bothering to tell her."

"Yes, I suppose he wouldn't be the first man in history to have pulled that stunt, unfortunately." Thomas frowned but then looked up at Elin with a twinkle in his eye.

"So, you're what then, a detective?"

"I don't know if I'd take it that far, but I work for a private eye."

"Oh, that's close enough! I would really need your help

finding someone," he said with a sly smile. "The man of my dreams!" He exclaimed and laughed heartily at his own joke, which made Elin start giggling too.

"I know what you mean. I've been looking for him myself, but there have only been dead-end leads so far."

"Cheers to that."

They clinked their glasses together. This afternoon was already turning out more pleasantly than Elin had anticipated.

CHAPTER 20

AIDAN WAS deep in his own thoughts as he strolled down Grev Turegatan. Drew had asked him so many times to seek out Morgan that he had finally caved in. He was actually a little bit curious himself why Morgan had gone so far as to tell Drew that he was coming to London and then just ghosted him. They had genuinely seemed to get along well. Maybe he was one of those people who goes through a real personality change as soon as they have had a couple of glasses and then just panic the day after. Aidan was not quite sure what to say to Morgan and hoped to himself that he would not be too upset having him just showing up at his door.

All the restaurants around Sturegallerian looked as vibrant and buzzing with activity as they had been when they had been staking them out months earlier. The only difference was the cold autumn rain and the biting wind trying to grab hold of his coat.

To his surprise, the front gate to Morgan's apartment building was unlocked. Dirt and wet leaves had gathered at the doorstep, preventing the door from closing properly. The staircase was elegant, and from the looks, built in the early 20th century, with marble floors and high ceilings—a far cry from his own home in Fruängen.

He decided to walk up the stairs. He had not had the time to work out much lately, so he was thankful for any opportunity to get some exercise. He lived by the philosophy that every step you took, every shopping bag carried home from the grocery store, all made a difference. He was still fit enough to sprint up the three flights of stairs without getting winded. Standing by the door of Morgan Lundin's apartment, it took him a few moments to understand what he was looking at. The blue and white plastic ribbon had a menacing familiarity. But it was not until he read the print that it actually sank in.

"*POLICE LINE DO NOT CROSS*"

The loud noise of the old elevator springing to life made him jump. He had been standing frozen to the floor by the door for minutes, trying to figure out what was going on. The elevator door opened, and an elderly lady stepped out and looked curiously at him.

"Good afternoon."

"Good afternoon, ma'am."

She walked up to the door next to Morgan and started scrambling around for the keys in her purse. Once she finally got them up, she was left standing with them in her hand for a moment before turning to Aidan again.

"What's your business here?"

She carried on before Aidan had a chance to answer.

"Did you know Mr. Lundin?"

"Yes, we're acquainted. I need to get in touch with him."

"Oh, dear. Haven't you heard? Such a dreadful business. Mr. Lundin has perished. Murder!"

CHAPTER 21

THOUGHTS WERE RUSHING through Aidan's head. For a while, he had been convinced that he would faint. The twenty-minute ride on the subway back to his apartment had felt like an eon. He had an overwhelming feeling that he had to do something but no idea what that would be. To his great relief, Gunvor was home in her apartment. She had given him a surprised look as she opened her front door but then listened carefully to his story.

"You should call the police. Hopefully, they can give you some information, and maybe they'll have questions for you too, seeing as you saw him so recently."

Gunvor wasted no time dialing the non-emergency number to the police and handed the phone over to Aidan. The officer on the phone turned out to be much more interested in Aidan's story than he had anticipated, and when they finally hung up, he hurried to call Drew and give him the bad news in person before the police would call and start asking questions.

The conversation was emotional, as expected. Drew's shock manifested itself with sobs and heartbroken wails.

"I knew something was wrong. He wouldn't just abandon me. He could have been the love of my life."

Aidan believed him. There was no doubt there had been something special about Morgan.

When the call finally ended, Aidan was exhausted. Even though he wanted to help Marie, he did not have another night out on the town left in him. He could not even bring himself to call her and cancel. He turned off his phone and collapsed on Guvnor's couch. He was sad for Morgan and sad that Drew had possibly lost the best chance of love he would ever have. But more than anything, he was overcome with the feeling that nothing is ever certain. You can go about your life, happy, dancing and drinking with your friends and the next day —dead.

Gunvor offered him a glass of single malt and then another one. He gave her a hug before he went back up to his own apartment. Nothing is ever certain.

CHAPTER 22
TUESDAY, NOVEMBER 3

GUNVOR HAD GATHERED everyone for a meeting at her apartment. She needed all the help she could get. Maybe someone had seen or heard something that could help the case without having realized it. Aidan, of course, was not part of the investigation but had been invited anyway for being a good thinking partner, and besides, maybe they could offer him some help on that little investigation he had going on his own.

She had spent the better part of the early afternoon trying to summarize her own observations and theories. No matter which way she looked at what little information they had been able to gather, she kept arriving at the same conclusion. Per Cedergren had met another woman and had no wish to be found. If there was any truth to his father's testament, this might just be another little adventure to Per. He would likely turn up soon enough, either to file for divorce or to come back to his old life, pretending that nothing had happened. Maybe his wife had turned a blind eye to his previous, less salient, slips, which made him bolder. Less careful.

The things Eva had said about Per being sensitive and

under a lot of pressure, while it might be true, did not seem like a plausible explanation for his disappearance in Gunvor's opinion. Per's father, Carl, for better or worse, seemed to have a more realistic view of the situation. Gunvor felt sorry for Eva, living in denial. She had many years of experience of it herself. Unfortunately, it was nothing strange or unusual. Just sad.

Elin was the first one to arrive. She did not have a bag or purse with her, so Gunvor assumed that she had stopped by her house on the way from school. Her curious nature drove her to make seemingly meaningless observations like this constantly, and she had an itch to ask Elin about it, but she knew it would just come across as nosey and controlling. After all, it really did not make any difference one way or the other. She also noticed that Elin looked a little pale. However, that probably was to be expected this time of year. Anyone that had not had the same luxury as Gunvor, of going away to a warmer climate for a couple of weeks in the fall, had every reason to look pale.

"We'll hold off with our speculations about the case until everyone is here if that's okay with you. Would you like some coffee?"

"Fair enough. Coffee sounds lovely, thanks."

While Gunvor loaded the new coffee maker and prepared a tray of turrón, a magnificent nougat she had brought from Spain, Elin asked her about the trip. Gunvor did not think that her days on the island made for much of a story. But when she saw how Elin dreamingly absorbed every little detail of the sunny vacation, she told her about their morning walks in flip-flops to the local bakery. Followed by trips to Amfi Beach and dips in the tepid, turquoise sea. Late dinners and wine at the neighboring restaurants. Sometimes tapas, beers, and televised football games in one of the bars at the plazas of Arguineguin.

"Oh, I can't believe I haven't mentioned this before, but you should go some time. Kjell has a spare room so you wouldn't have to pay for a hotel, and the flights can be really cheap if you book at the right time."

"Kjell actually offered for both David and me to come over when he was here. It would be great to go sometime."

Gunvor sent Kjell a loving thought. She really had been lucky to meet someone so thoughtful.

"It's just hard to find the right time to go, I'm still in school for a while, and I don't know how long David's training will be."

"Okay, but believe me, if you get a chance, it's well worth it. And you can go at any time of the year. It's always summer over there."

The doorbell rang. David had barely gotten through the door before Gunvor started telling them both about Aidan's shocking experience the day before.

"Oh god, that's so sad. That's really horrible." Elin almost teared up.

"Shit." David could not think of anything else to say.

"I just wanted to let you know before he gets here. In case he's acting strange or something, which I don't think he will. But let's not overwhelm him with questions and just let him choose if he wants to talk about it, okay?"

Elin and David both nodded in agreement.

Soon, they were all gathered around her kitchen table once again. Gunvor was delighted, despite everything. The disappointment of not having made much progress in the investigation so far was curbed by the fact that she was surrounded by her best friends. Except for Kjell, of course. She felt the stab of a guilty conscience for having left him alone. But this was important work, and she would be back by his side soon enough.

"Beloved friends. I want to thank you all so much for helping me out with this investigation. Now, where do we begin?"

"I'd like to go first if that's okay."

The apartment had been buzzing with activity when Aidan walked through the door. David was telling some story from his training. Gunvor had decided she wanted to treat everyone to some Ron Miel and was busy trying to find four tiny glasses. It was not until they got seated that they noticed something seemed off about Aidan. Gunvor thought that it was only natural, given his discovery the day before, but she asked him anyway.

"Aidan, are you okay?"

Elin and David paused their bantering and looked at him.

"Something has happened."

"Yes, I took the liberty of telling them before you got here." Gunvor patted him tenderly on the shoulder.

"Not that, something else."

Aidan was visibly upset, and a grave silence quickly replaced the warm atmosphere that had occupied the apartment a few minutes earlier.

"You know I've been helping this woman, Marie. We're trying to find her friend, who has disappeared."

"Yes. Seb, right?"

"Right. So, on Sunday, Marie and I were looking for Seb at Patricia. You know, the nightclub on the boat down by Södermälarstrand?"

He looked around the table to make sure everyone was following.

"And we didn't find Seb, but I talked to someone. Well,

actually, I talked with his friend because he was too busy on the dance floor. But either way, this guy had been in a relationship with Seb."

He took a deep breath to keep his composure.

"He was murdered on his way home that same night."

Everyone stared at Aidan with alarmed expressions.

"Wait, who was killed?" Elin spoke first.

"Was Seb killed, or the guy you talked to?" David asked with a puzzled look.

"How do you know he was killed?" Gunvor said, before realizing that they should probably give Aidan a chance to answer one question before asking him the next one.

"No, no. The guy that had an affair with Seb was murdered. I never spoke to him directly, but I saw him. His friend was telling me about him. I saw the headlines in this morning's paper, but they didn't mention Patricia or anything, and I was in a hurry, so..." He trailed off. "His name was Alexander, by the way." He got quiet again. His thoughts were flying to and fro, and it was a struggle keeping up with them. "It wasn't until just now, on my way back from work, that I realized what had happened because they've posted his picture."

"But how? Why? Elin asked as she was trying to load the article.

"Head trauma, whatever that means. They found him floating by the quay."

"Imagine being killed just for walking home. This world never fails to disappoint," David muttered.

"Do you think it might have anything to do with the case?" Gunvor's curiosity had already outgrown her dismay.

"That wouldn't make much sense. But nothing seems to make sense right now, so what do I know. Earlier that night, I saw a man I recognized from at least one of the other venues where we've been looking for Seb. Marie had talked to him earlier, and he wouldn't tell her anything. I just had a feeling about him, so I decided to try and talk with him anyway. Alone. Turns out, he does know Seb. He told me Seb has something he's got to do, and Marie can't know about it. Isn't that strange? Oh my god, what if Seb is out on a killing spree? And he killed Morgan and Alexander, and now he's going to kill me?

"Okay, wow. Take a deep breath. I understand that you're upset, but a person vanishing, to then go on a killing spree. And also telling his friends about it? And the friends won't go to the police, but they're hinting about it to strangers in a night-club? I literally couldn't come up with a more unlikely scenario if I tried. We don't know anything about this, Alexander. There are plenty of ways to get yourself killed, unfortunately. And as far as Seb goes, I'll admit that it is strange about his friend, but I'm sure it's nothing sinister."

Gunvor wished she had known how shook up Aidan was and felt bad for not having offered to let him sleep on the couch the night before. He had probably needed the company.

"Maybe he's getting together a surprise for her. Does she have a big birthday coming up?" Elin said in an attempt to steer the conversation back on track.

"Yes. Good thinking. There's almost always a perfectly natural explanation. He probably hasn't realized how upset his disappearance would make her. This guy that you talked to, Seb's friend. Does he have a name?"

"I never thought to ask...."

"Ok, that's fine. We'll call him John Doe, for now, to avoid any confusion. So, since he claims to know Seb and his whereabouts, he is obviously a person we'd like to talk to again.

Although you said Marie had already tried to talk to him before, so we can't rule out the possibility that he just got tired of you two asking him questions and just made up a story to wind you up." Gunvor continued.

Aidan scratched his head thoughtfully for a moment before he spoke.

"I guess not, but I have to say, that's really not the vibe I got from him at all. But, strangely, he seems to know who Marie is, while she doesn't seem to have any idea who he is."

"I don't think that's too surprising. It's pretty natural to tell your friends about your other friends, so there is nothing odd about John Doe knowing about Marie. And when we spoke earlier, I remember you telling me that Marie wanted nothing to do with Seb's party lifestyle, so that would explain why he hasn't told her about John Doe."

"Oh... Yes, I suppose you're right." Aidan nodded in agreement, but then a miserable expression came back like a dark shadow over his face. "I'm really having problems seeing things clearly. My mind feels so clouded. I have this picture that won't go away. As I left Patricia, I thought I saw this John Doe guy again on the deck. He just stood there in the darkness, looking down at me. I don't know what it means. Or if it even means anything. But I just can't let it go."

"It's probably just your mind connecting it to the murder, making it seem more menacing than it was. But we'll look into any possibility." Gunvor got up from her chair to put more Turrón on the tray.

"I guess I have myself to blame for wanting your life. Now I've ended up in this whole mess, and I just want out."

"It's part of the job." Gunvor smiled. "You'll get past it; the thrill of the mystery beats anything. Even this. But I think it's time we started working both cases, all of us together."

"Can I just say one thing." Elin didn't wait for an answer before she continued. "Could it be that the disappearances are linked together somehow? I mean Per and Seb. Maybe I'm just grasping for straws here, but they both hang out at gay bars, right? In both cases, there's been someone assuring us they're fine and will be back soon. Per's dad and this John Doe. Isn't that a little unusual? Maybe they're together?"

"Gay bars?" Gunvor was confused.

"Right. Urban Deli?" She turned to David. "You noticed, right?"

"I didn't think it meant anything." The question made David feel awkward. He lied, not to seem unaware. He had thought that it was just that old man that had been harassing him. And possibly the bartender."

"A lot of people just come there to eat. But the bar is apparently kind of a hookup place for gay men. At least that's what I've been told. I met a man there yesterday, who was very helpful. He'd seen Per there a lot but wasn't sure if he'd just been there for the food or not. But he's promised to look into it and check with the other patrons."

"That's great work, Elin. We'll put that in the notes. But I personally doubt that they've disappeared together. From what I've found out so far, it seems more likely that Per was there to buy something from this Felix. You wouldn't believe how common drug use is among these senior management types. A lot of them are using just to cope with the workload. And in many cases, you could never tell. I've read that they are micro-dosing cocaine or even LSD just to boost efficiency and creativity without getting noticeably high. As a performance enhancer."

"But if Felix is a drug dealer, do you think he will help us out or even admit that he knows Per?" David was relieved that he had been let off the hook so easily about the whole gay bar thing.

"If he does know Per, I think we could probably find out. The biggest problem now is finding him. This is really a strange case we've stumbled upon." Gunvor gave everyone a refill on their Ron Miel and ate a piece of the Turrón before she went on. "I could always ask Eva if Per ever hangs out at gay bars. He could have gay friends or just, you know, get on well with that crowd, even though neither his father nor wife exactly strikes me as the progressive type. What about your case Aidan, do you have any suggestions on how to move forward there?"

"How about you meet Marie? I'm sure you could ask her things that I haven't even thought about, that could give us some kind of new information. And if it turns out that Per is hanging out at gay bars, maybe we could start staking out places together. Or maybe take turns. Going out every night is starting to take its toll on me."

"Sure thing. Will you call her and set something up after we're done here?"

"Will do."

"Great. I really think finding John Doe again should be a priority. Try to feel him out a little. It might be a good idea to do that without Marie, so I suggest you and David get on that. Elin, I'd like you to continue working Urban Deli if that's okay. See if your contact knows anything about Felix, or any drug distribution going on there."

Elin nodded eagerly.

"Sounds good. There's no school in the morning tomorrow, so I could actually go there tonight."

"I have some pictures of Alexander and John Doe on my phone. I pretended to take selfies when Marie went to the bathroom. The photo of Seb is on her phone, but I'll ask her to send it over when I call her later."

"Good. I'll get in touch with Eva and try Felix's apartment again. Is everyone happy with this plan? Should we meet up again tomorrow for evaluation?"

After Elin and David had left, Aidan stuck around for a bit. Gunvor opened up a good bottle of Rioja while she let a pot of tomato-sauce simmer on the stove. He needed to get all his thoughts on the two murders off his chest, and she welcomed the company.

CHAPTER 23

ELIN WAS TORMENTED by a massive hangover and had spent most of the day feeling queasy and a little sorry for herself. When she took the first sip of her beer at Urban Deli, she finally started feeling a little better. For a while, she had been worried that she might throw up at Gunvor's place. Luckily, she had gotten through the coffee and the nougat, and the liquor had for better or worse curbed the feeling somewhat.

She had been hoping that Thomas would be at the restaurant and looked around the tables carefully when she arrived, but so far, there was no sign of him. It was really remarkable how well they had been getting along. He had told her his life story, with honesty and much detail. He thought it was a tragic one. To her, it seemed full of excitement and adventures. He had grown up in a time when homosexuality was not talked about, other than as a sick and shameful deviation. That painful time of alienation had, in all its despair, given life to a strong sub-culture in the cities at that time, which Thomas had been a part of. Elin, who had never really had a sense of unity with anyone, except maybe now with the Fruängen Bureau, had romanticized the idea. Yet she was disturbed by the thought of not being accepted in society and even being forced to hide part of your identity.

Elin finished her beer quickly. It scared her how good it made her feel. The hangover that had made her call in sick from school was now almost completely gone. Maybe she should call in sick tomorrow as well? It seemed a bit suspicious to only be sick for one day anyway. If she did, it would not be a problem if she got a little hungover again. With that in mind, she ordered a refill. She was annoyed that she never thought of exchanging numbers with Thomas. Perhaps he would show up later in the evening.

CHAPTER 24

DAVID DID NOT IDENTIFY as homophobic, per se. He had no problem as long as they kept it to themselves, and he was not one of those dudes who got grossed out by seeing a gay couple hold hands or show even kiss in public. What's it to him? However, he was not comfortable sitting alone at the bar at Side Track. Not comfortable at all. He had spent quite a few nights at the place next door, Black and Brown. It was one of those pubs, like Västertorps Hjärta or Parma, where the clientele mostly consisted of men who called their friends bro and worked with sales or some kind of manual labor.

Despite the close proximity, Side Track could not be further from Black and Brown in every other sense. People here were less—ordinary. Dressed up. Not the kind of clothes you would wear to work. Unless, of course, you worked as a bartender at Side Track. David had ordered his beer from a man in his forties wearing a long blonde wig, fake lashes, and a sparkling silver dress.

Aidan had called earlier to ask if it would be okay if he sat this one out. He did not want to let David down and was prepared to go with him, but he had been through a lot in the last couple of days and did not feel quite fit for another night out.

It was a Tuesday. Slowest night of the week. Patricia was closed, but this place supposedly shared much of the same crowd. Perhaps that was the reason that they were so busy after all. David had been lucky to have found a seat at the bar.

Aidan sent over the photos he had taken at Patricia. They were a little blurry, but David thought he would probably be able to recognize John Doe if he were to show up.

David downed his first gin and tonic and ordered a second one. It was expensive, but worth it. Looking around the room again, he caught sight of a man his own age. There was something familiar about him. The man suddenly looked up, and their eyes met for a brief second. A gentle and flirty shimmer woke to life in the man's eyes. David quickly looked away.

CHAPTER 25

IT WAS after 10 p.m. when Aidan left Gunvor's apartment. Since they had been drinking wine, she decided that both her phone call to Eva and her visit to Felix would have to wait until the morning. As she was preparing for bed, a little disappointed in herself, she suddenly came up with a brilliant idea. At least, it would be brilliant if it worked. She picked up her phone to call her nephew. Johan had always been a night owl and would probably still be up.

Gunvor never had kids of her own. Johan was the closest she had. She and her sister only spoke occasionally. But she saw Johan, if not often, at least regularly. They had always had a strong bond.

"Hey! How are you? It's been a while. Are you home from your trip yet?"

Just hearing his voice warmed Gunvor's heart.

"Hi, dear. Yes, I'm home and working on a new case."

"Of course you are. You wouldn't waste your life on leisure and that sort of nonsense, would you?"

Gunvor laughed.

"And I'm guessing you're calling because you need me to do something? I'd be more than happy to help, of course."

Gunvor felt ashamed when she realized that he was right. She had called him just to ask for a favor. Again.

"Well, yes, I'm sorry. But actually, it's your wife I need this time. She still works for SL, right?"

She had discussed work countless times with Johan's wife, Helena. SL, the commonly used abbreviation for Stockholms Lokaltrafik, handled all public transports within the region. But for some reason, she could never remember exactly what it was Helena did. Some kind of project management? She cursed herself. For all her expertise at gathering information, it felt ridiculous and ignorant not being able to remember. It was just that, sometimes, when information did not really seem to be relevant to anything she was doing, her mind tended to start wandering.

"Yeah, she's still there. What do you need from SL?"

"I was wondering if she would be able to access passenger-lists for the ferries to Nämndö last weekend? I assume you can't check cash payments, but can you check people who bought tickets with credit cards or people who used personal travel cards? I need to know when, or actually if, someone left the island. And if he was even there in the first place."

"Gotcha. Helena has gone to bed, but I'll ask her first thing in the morning. I think she could probably get access to that information, but I have a feeling it would be very illegal to share that kind of information."

"Well, obviously, we can't have her getting in trouble, but it's not illegal to ask, is it?"

"Ever heard of incitement?" Johan laughed.

After they hung up, Gunvor treated herself to another nightcap. She felt like she deserved it after coming up with an idea like that. She blew out the candles and walked up to the bedroom window, looked up at the full moon, and promised herself she would become a better listener.

CHAPTER 26

DAVID COULD NOT THINK of a time when he had been more uncomfortable. Alone and surrounded by men who wanted other men and women that would not even spare him a look. How could he possibly conceal how out of place he was?

"Hello."

The voice belonged to the man he had recognized earlier. Warm, brown eyes looked curiously at him.

"Hi."

"You look a bit lost. Are you new here? Or have you just ended up in the wrong place?"

"A little bit of both, I suppose. I'm on the lookout for a missing person that I think might be a regular here."

"Oh, how fun! Can I help?"

David felt a creeping panic from even speaking to anyone at this place, but at the same time, he really needed all the help he could get. He got out his phone and showed the picture of Per Cedergren.

"Do you know him?"

The young man studied the picture closely before answering.

"I sort of recognize him, don't know him, though."

When David pulled up the picture of Alexander, the man's smile faded.

"Oh, don't tell me you're looking for him. Haven't you heard what happened to him?"

"Yes, I know. Sorry. I'm actually looking for two missing people. But I only have a photo of the first guy I showed you. His name is Per. The other guy I'm looking for—Seb—supposedly had an affair with Alexander. You don't happen to know anything about that? I don't know much about him except he's in his mid-fifties."

"Okay, well, I didn't know Alexander too well. The only one I've seen him really hang around with a lot is this guy Paul, but he's young-ish, and I'm pretty sure they're only like friends."

"Alright, thanks. I've got one more picture. This guy is not missing, that I know of at least, but we think he's a friend of Seb, and I'd like to get in touch with him."

David held up the photo of the man they had dubbed John Doe.

"Oh yeah, I've seen him around. I think he is a friend of the first guy you showed me. Peter, right?"

"You mean Per? Really, they're friends? Are you sure?"

"I'm pretty sure, at least I've seen them together."

"Do you know his name?"

"No, what do I care about some old guy's name? I've just seen them around."

"Do you remember if there was a third guy with them when you saw them?" David thought that, since Seb knew

John Doe, and apparently John Doe knew Per, maybe that meant all three of them were friends.

"Yeah, maybe, I don't know." He gave David a smile that could only be interpreted as flirtatious. David got uncomfortable again and was not sure how to handle the situation. He was thankful for the help, but the flirting was unbearable to him. The man seemed to notice and changed his expression.

"Hampus." He held out his hand, offering a handshake.

For a moment, David contemplated giving a false name. To avoid any evidence that he had ever been there. What if it somehow got back to his friends? But before opening his mouth, he realized that it might just cause more trouble. What if he had to get in touch with Hampus later on for more questioning and was not able to remember what name he had given him?

"David."

"So. How do you feel about this then?"

"What do you mean?" The delay of David's answer made it obvious he knew exactly what he meant.

"To be here? Standing here with me?"

"I'm grateful for your help."

"You know that's not what I meant. You're new here. I know what it's like. Trust me."

David doubted that Hampus knew what it was like for him.

"Seriously, I'm just here for work. Can you tell me anything else about these men? Have you seen them anywhere else than here? Do they come here a lot or just sometimes?" David tried desperately to sound as matter-of-fact and professional as possible.

"Boooring. If you dance with me, maybe I'll remember more." Hampus gave him another flirtatious smile.

"But..." The thought made David's mouth dry up.

"Oh my god, dude, I'm messing with you. Although I've got to say sometimes, I really wish I had the same conviction that some of you heterosexuals do, that every gay guy so desperately wants me."

This made David blush with embarrassment, and they both laughed.

"I've seen them here and over at Patricia. That's it. But I don't really hang out too much at any other gay bars. As far as I remember, they're just two old men that sit and drink together. I thought maybe they were an old couple, but I've never seen them make out or anything like that, so they might just be friends. I haven't paid them that much attention, to be honest."

By now, the venue's atmosphere was really starting to take off, and David realized it would be impossible to maintain any kind of constructive conversation. Luckily, the information he had already gotten was more than he had expected. If John Doe knew Per, maybe all they had to do to crack this whole case was to find him.

"Listen, thanks again for all your help. I have an early morning, so I need to get going."

"No worries, I love a good mystery. I hope you'll get over the trauma of visiting this scary gay-bar." Hampus blew him a kiss and disappeared onto the dance floor.

CHAPTER 27

WHEN THOMAS finally walked through the doors of Urban Deli, Elin's heart skipped a beat. She had not realized how happy she would be to see him again. His face cracked up in a big smile as they embraced in a warm hug.

"Oh, I'm so happy to see you again!" She almost felt a little embarrassed. But after just one night of conversations, he had proved to be more of a role model and father figure than her own father had ever been.

"Me too, dear. Me too." He patted her gently on the cheek. "How are you feeling today? We had way too much to drink last night, didn't we?"

"I know, but it was nice."

"Indeed, very nice."

They found a couple of empty seats at the far end of the bar and ordered a beer each.

"How is your adventure going, dear? Have you found any good clues?"

Elin smiled.

"I might have. I've been assigned to ask you a few questions tonight. I just want to say, though, and I'm sorry if this is cringe-worthy, but I just wanted to say that our talk yesterday really meant something to me. It was so inspiring to hear your story of being alienated and having to navigate people's prejudice. I can't compare my own experiences to that, of course, but I haven't really had many friends, and I've had really low self-esteem. I'm lucky to have made friends with Gunvor and David and Aidan, but they're all very different from me and. I know everyone has their own problems and all, but it's been really great to meet you because I feel like you were like me once, and you were able to rise above it. That gives me hope that maybe I will too."

"Oh darling, can't you see that you already have? Look at you, with your investigations and making friends with pathetic old men." They both laughed.

"Seriously, though, Elin. You're doing great, even if it doesn't always feel like it, and I'm the one that should be thankful to have met you."

He took her hand, and they both contemplated in silence for a moment.

"Oh dear, it's not every day you get to be this emotional, is it? Can I get you a small glass of single malt to celebrate?"

He waited for the bartender to return to his place behind the register after serving them before he continued.

"Now. How about those questions you had for me?"

"Ok. This is kind of a sensitive subject, so I'm hoping you'll be honest. I'm not looking to bust anyone. I'm just looking for a missing person. Or two, actually."

Thomas raised his eyebrows.

"Blimey! They're two now? What happened?"

"I know, I know. At first, I thought they might have gone away together, but apparently, that's very unlikely. Gunvor says they are over 6000 missing person reports in Sweden every year, so we just happened to get two cases at once."

"No kidding? That sounds like a lot of missing people."

"It's true. But most of them turn up after a day or two, luckily."

"So, what's your question?"

"One of the employees here, Felix, has gone missing."

"Oh, Felix is the other missing person?"

"Well, actually, no."

"So, wait… there are three missing people now?"

Thomas rolled his eyes dramatically.

"Well, technically. But we're only assigned to find two. The thing is, there have been indications that Per knows Felix. And that Felix might be selling drugs. We don't have any evidence for either claim, but we're trying to check out whether there might be a connection to the disappearance. So, my question to you is, do you know Felix? And if so, do you know if he is selling drugs? And do you know if Per Cedergren or anyone else here is using drugs?"

Thomas sighed deeply.

"I guess you could say it's something that is going around. Some people are only using sporadically, and some get stuck. There are so many lost souls out there, you know. Even though the acceptance and respect for the LGBTQ community is better than it has been, a lot of us are still struggling. I guess you kind of know firsthand that alcohol can be a pretty convenient way to get away from your burdens for a moment. Some people have been getting into other habits. GHB, cocaine, crystal meth. They're all pretty common around here. I've seen too many friends succumb to them one way or another. It's really heartbreaking to see people trying to get rid of one demon by running into the arms of another. I've used my fair share of cocaine back in the days, but consider myself lucky to have been able to get out in time."

Thomas' face got sadder and sadder as he spoke, and Elin was struck by remorse for bringing up the subject.

"I'm so sorry; I didn't mean for you to get upset."

"Oh, it's quite alright, darling. It's actually quite nice to be able to talk about it. No use just carrying around all that stuff inside you. I've made many silly mistakes in my life, but I've been lucky to get through relatively unscathed. These days I'm just worried about all the young folks, not knowing what they're getting themselves into."

"So, do you know anything about Felix?"

"He's that young lad who works here, correct? After all these years, I know most of the staff by name. He's very nice, but I don't know about any drugs. I think everyone here is quite aware of my opinion on drugs, so if he does sell them, I don't think he'd offer me to buy. Besides, I know that the bar manager shares my view, and he is quite attentive, so if Felix is actually selling drugs, it would have to be very discreet." Thomas smiled faintly. "But certainly, especially on the weekends, it's quite clear that some people here are using something, and if memory serves me right, that includes your Per. But that goes for pretty much every bar in the city, so I'm not sure how helpful that is to you.

"That's plenty helpful, thanks! And Cheers!

Elin was happy that they now, thanks to her, had more or less confirmed that Per was using drugs, which meant that the Felix lead was still worth pursuing. Whether it had anything to do with his disappearance was a question for later.

CHAPTER 28
WEDNESDAY, NOVEMBER 4

"WHY AM I even paying you? First, you're telling me he's cheating on me, and now it's all filth and drugs? If I've told you once, I've told you a thousand times—my husband is suffering from depression, and I need you to find him. What's so hard to understand? You know, at first, I was happy that a woman would lead the investigation because I thought you might actually listen, but I guess the joke is on me."

Gunvor was holding her phone at a distance from her ear to avoid the full force of Eva's piercing voice.

"It's always tricky to find a missing person, especially if the person has gone missing on his or her own accord. I am truly sorry to have upset you, but in order to find him, I need to find out as much as possible about him and then figure out where he might have gone to."

"I've told you he's depressed."

"And I'm grateful that you've shared that with me. Unfortunately, that's not enough information to find him. I need to map out his habits to get a better sense of where he could be."

"Yes, that is working out just fabulously for you, isn't it?

You still haven't got a clue where he is, and you keep calling me with more and more exceedingly ridiculous theories. Just do your job and find him! And don't bother calling me unless you have any actual information or questions that aren't nonsense."

The rage lingered in the air long after Eva had hung up the line. Gunvor sighed and noted to herself that this investigation had proven to be far harder to navigate than she had anticipated. After some thinking, she decided that it was time for another chat with the patriarch, Carl. Maybe he could shed some light on his son's secret habits.

CHAPTER 29

AIDAN SLEPT UNTIL EARLY AFTERNOON. Even though the sleep had been light and filled with feverish dreams, he felt more well-rested than he had in the last couple of days. He went down to Gunvor's as agreed upon the night before, and they shared breakfast, as usual, consisting of coffee and a protein shake, although lunch would have probably been more appropriate.

He had two crucial calls to make. One was to Marie, who he had never gotten around to calling the night before. The second one was to find out the date and location for Morgan's funeral. He had promised he would ask the family if Drew could attend. Even though they had been deprived of a chance to really get to know each other, Drew was devastated to have lost what he now referred to as his best chance of true love in life. He hoped that he would at least have an opportunity to pay his respects to Morgan's family and have a last farewell. Since Morgan's last name, Lundin, was relatively common, Aidan was not sure how to go about finding the right person to call, so Gunvor offered to help him find out the details while he called Marie to set up a meeting.

Marie picked up after the first signal. She must have already had the phone in her hand when it started ringing. To Aidan's surprise, she did not sound very alarmed or even interested when he told her about the two deaths. Her coolness seemed to become more pronounced every time they spoke. It scared him. The fact that such an egocentric and disconnected person could have such an effect on him was a mystery.

She was not in the least impressed by his offer to introduce her Gunvor.

"I don't see what good that would do." She even sounded a little agitated. "Listen, I appreciate your help. But this is about my friend and me. You have no right to take matters into your own hands and start gossiping about us."

Aidan struggled to contain himself, but his tone still had a sharp edge when he replied.

"I haven't been gossiping. I've spoken in confidence with a close friend who has expertise in these kinds of investigations. She is offering to take a look at your case for free. If I were in your shoes, I'd be thrilled."

There was a long silence, but Aidan had no intention of being the first one to speak. Once again, he was struck by the suspicion that she was more emotionally entangled with Seb than she was willing to admit. Maybe he had just wanted a break from her, and that was why he left. He did not get any further with his train of thought before Marie broke the silence.

"But isn't she just spying on cheating husbands and things? This is nothing juicy like that."

"She handles all kinds of cases." Aidan did not think it

would be constructive to point out that Gunvor was fairly new to the field. "But if you don't want help, I won't force you. I just thought because Gunvor is working on a similar case anyway...."

Marie didn't let him finish.

"But it's not a similar case, is it? It's just a waste of my time. And yours, if you want to help me."

Aidan thought that she might actually be right. Not that she would know. He had not even gotten a chance to tell her about Gunvor's case. Marie was just her usual stubborn self. But it was true that they did not have any real indication that the cases were connected or even similar. Then again, he had been too shaken up to be able to focus on the meeting and everything that had been said the day before. He did not ask her for the photo of Seb. It seemed like it would just make her more upset.

"Aidan?"

Suddenly her voice was much softer.

"Yes?"

"I'm sorry about your friend. That his..." She trailed off, like if she was searching her brain for a fitting word but went on without settling on one. "...got killed. I met him too, remember? He seemed like a nice man."

"Thanks."

"Let me know if there's anything I can do."

Hearing her voice so tender now, the coolness from the start of the conversation had completely vanished, making Aidan suddenly yearn to look into those beautiful eyes once again.

"Yes. I don't know. Thanks."

"Are you coming out with me tonight?"

"Sure."

Aidan hung up, convinced he had just gotten himself into more trouble.

CHAPTER 30

IN THE EARLY AFTERNOON, Gunvor received an email from Helena. She was adamant that the contents attached—several passenger manifests from the archipelago ferries—could under no circumstances be leaked or traced back to her, or it would cost her both her job and freedom.

Thank you, darling! You're a lifesaver, and I won't tell a soul about this. I owe you one!

The manifests were sorted by date and time—departures from Saltsjöbadenand Stavnäs calling at Nämdö for the whole weekend Per had supposedly spent at the summerhouse. Each line of the list included a name and a combination of digits that looked like they might be social security numbers. Gunvor could not figure out whether these were passengers paying with credit cards, or registered travel cards, or both. But she was hopeful that she would get some useful information out of them. She scrolled through the manifests beginning with the fares from the Sunday, the week before, and focused on the list of people traveling from Nämdö back to Stockholm.

It did not take long to find the name Per Cedergren on one

of the lists. That meant he had gone to visit the house after all. She tried to understand why he would have even bothered to go there if he was planning to disappear somewhere else anyway. Maybe he needed time to organize a more extended trip with a mistress. A trip that took them far away from the ever-watching eyes of his wife and his father? Did he want solitude before he went off on his adventure? Time to distance himself? Rid himself of a guilty conscience?

Using Per's column in the manifest as a reference, she confirmed that the digits were, in fact, social security numbers. That meant the job of identifying any other passenger on that list, someone like a potential lover, would be much easier. Gunvor started sorting through the female names on the list. Most of them were women over sixty. She did not bother looking any closer at them. Not that she thought that Per would mind an age difference as long as he was the older one.

Two were under twelve years of age. She did not bother with them either. That left three women with ages between thirty and fifty, but for each one, there was a male passenger with the same surname, which made her assume that they were married couples traveling together. Of course, they could be siblings or cousins, but it made equally little sense to bring the family to a love affair. That left only one name—Vera Rosén, age sixteen. Gunvor was quietly hoping that her suspicions were not correct.

One thing that pointed away from a connection between the two of them was the fact that Vera Rosén had paid for her own ticket. If Per had gotten himself such a young mistress, then it would make much more sense for him to have paid for the ticket. On the other hand, Gunvor was not quite sure how the manifest was set up, and Per might have given Vera money to buy a personal travel card.

She looked up Vera Rosén online and found that she was registered at an address in Sundsvall. That was halfway across the country. How would a successful businessman end up with a sixteen-year-old girl from Sundsvall? Even in the era of internet dating, it seemed strange.

There were three phone numbers registered to the address. One number belonged to someone named Ove Granberg, and the other two to an Annika Rosén. Gunvor assumed that it was Vera's mother. That probably meant that one of the numbers belonged to Vera and one to the mother. Gunvor dialed the first number.

"Annika Rosén speaking."

"Hi. My name is Gunvor Ström. I'm a private investigator based in Stockholm. I was hoping to speak with Vera Rosén."

"What's this about?" The woman on the other end of the line sounded suspicious.

"Are you Vera's mother?"

"I am. What is this about, please?"

"I'm looking for a missing person, and from the passenger manifest, I can see that your daughter was traveling on the same ferry from Nämndö last Sunday. I wanted to ask her if she might have seen something. Were you accompanying her on her trip?"

Gunvor realized that a sixteen-year-old kid was not likely to tell her mom that she was traveling to the big city to date a man in his fifties. She wondered what excuse she could have come up with to go to Stockholm alone.

"No, I wasn't. She was there visiting her dad. But she's usually devoured by her phone, like most of her generation, so I doubt she has seen anything of interest to you."

"I understand. Would you mind if I give her a call?"

"Yes, I would, actually. I'll ask her myself. If she's seen anything, I will let you know."

Gunvor cursed herself for having asked permission to call Vera.

"Okay. Thank you for your time."

Gunvor hung up and let out a deep sigh. She could not get herself to call the child against the mother's wishes. At least it did not seem to be a lead in the right direction. It was pretty obvious that Vera was not the secret lover of an older missing man, but just a girl visiting her dad for the weekend. And the woman had been right. Not only teens but practically everyone these days spent most of their time looking at their phones. It was not likely that Vera would have noticed Per on the ferry, even less whether he had been traveling alone or not.

CHAPTER 31

DAVID HAD CALLED IN SICK. He really liked his training, but sometimes it was just too slow. It made him restless. He had always thought of himself as a slow learner, but to his surprise, this training had come very easily to him. Now, instead, he was struggling with keeping his attention focused on the class. So, he had decided to take a day off. Another part of the reason was that he was pretty tired from the night before, and he knew he had to spend another night out. It was important that he was on high alert, not miss any vital clues. He hoped Aidan would not bail on him again.

He took a look around the kitchen and confirmed that his mom had neglected the grocery shopping as usual. After a moment of contemplation, he saw that he would not be able to come up with a good breakfast using the ingredients at hand—capers, butter, and ketchup. He put on his shoes and jacket and headed down to the shopping center.

He had been spending more and more of his student loans on groceries, not that he minded. He had been trying to cook too. Recipes that he found online. Even his mom, who usually kept to coffee and Marlboros when she was home, had tried some of his food. She assured him that the food they provided for her at the residential home for the elderly, where she worked, was quite enough.

He stopped to exchange a few words with some friends who were smoking cigarettes by the benches in the middle of the center, as usual, before his hunger forced him to head on to one of the two grocery stores nearby. Just as he picked up the shopping basket, he saw a familiar face. At first, he was not quite able to place it. But as it sank in, he started to panic. It was Hampus, the man from the gay bar.

Luckily Hampus seemed occupied deciding on a brand of rye bread, which gave David a chance to return the basket and flee out the doors quickly, and across the square outside over to the rivaling grocery store. But he knew that was only a temporary solution.

When they had met the night before, he had thought that there was something vaguely familiar about him. The possibility that he would live in the same neighborhood had not crossed his mind for a second. Now he realized that he must have seen him on the subway or at the shopping center. Not that he was checking out other guys. But if you saw someone in Fruängen that you did not know, you looked twice. And you did not just welcome anyone with open arms.

Maybe they had laughed at Hampus, David and his friends, or even taunted him. No, Hampus would have recognized him the night before if they had done something like that. It could not be that bad.

What if David had stopped and chatted a little longer with his friends and Hampus had come out of the store and recognized him? Maybe even stopped to chat? Blown him another kiss? A chill went down his spine.

David had already lived through a mild trauma when Gunvor had hacked his social media accounts and made troll posts in his name. It had been before they knew each other, and Gunvor had done it as revenge for David bullying Elin. He had long ago come to terms with the fact that he had it coming. But his friends had given him a hard time for quite a while after that, and under no circumstances did he want to become a laughingstock again. With those posts fresh in mind, everyone would lose their respect for him.

CHAPTER 32

ELIN STAYED in bed for a long time after she had woken up. She had decided to skip school once again. There was just too much stuff going on. Exciting stuff. She would not be able to keep her focus at school anyway.

Despite all the horrible things that had gone down in the last days, the two nights at Urban Deli, when she had gotten to know Thomas, had been magical. She had actually opened up to another person in a way she had never thought she would. And she had done it without hesitation. It was so strange. The only older man she ever knew was her violent father. She had not seen him since her parents divorced almost ten years ago.

The only thing he had left behind was a lingering distrust towards men. Not everyone, of course. Aidan was always nice and helpful. But he was really Gunvor's friend. And David had turned out to be a good friend, in the end. He would do anything for her. But deep heart-to-heart talks were not his thing.

Thomas had listened to her for hours. He had let her talk about all those things she had needed to talk about for so long

—moments of anguish and anxiety, the longing to belong, and the grief of being alienated.

In that very short period of time, she had let him in closer than any other person in her life. At the end of the second night, partly to her own surprise, she spurted out the words.

"I wish you had been my dad."

To her horror, Thomas started to cry. She wondered if she had offended him by making him feel old. She knew that he was struggling with aging and cursed herself for being so insensitive.

Instead, she heard him saying, "Me too, darling. Me too."

CHAPTER 33

DAVID FINALLY GOT his nerves under control. He knew that the situation demanded him to act as the detective he wanted to become. He would not even be much of a security guard if he ran and hid at the first sign of trouble.

He waited just inside the entrance of Coop until he saw Hampus walk out across the square. When Hampus made a right and began strolling down the pedestrian street, David snuck out and hurried across the square and onto the parking lot on the other side of the building. If Hampus did not stop at any of the other stores, he would soon turn up by the fountain at the far end of the building. The problem was that there was not really any place for David to hide while still being able to get an overview of the area and the many different paths leading out from it, so it would be difficult to keep track of Hampus. He decided to crouch down behind a parked car and pretended to tie the laces of the Nikes he still wore, although the temperature was now below freezing.

David peeked out carefully from behind the car before he got up. Hampus was nowhere to be seen. He wondered if he had been hiding behind the car for too long or if Hampus was just really slow. He walked at a rapid pace towards the fountain, looking in every direction. Suddenly, he saw Hampus just as he was disappearing up a set of stairs. David waited until he was completely out of sight and then quickly followed. At the top of the stairs was another smaller parking lot. The lot led to the subway station and a couple of small businesses, including a fishmonger and a café where David's mom had sometimes treated him to a soda and a piece of cake for his birthdays when he was a kid, to the right, and onto Elsa Brännström's Street through the residential neighborhood to the left. Hampus had taken a left turn, and when David caught a glimpse of him again, he was just passing the car repair shop on the next block. David kept as much of a distance as he could without losing him again. He did not want to risk a confrontation.

Hampus cut across the street and walked up Hanna Paulin's street. When David saw him enter the first apartment building on the right side of the street, he was content and strolled back to the shopping center. He did not know exactly why he had followed Hampus, but he just felt more in control, knowing where he lived. Besides, he was something of a witness, so it was good to be able to reach him should the need arise.

CHAPTER 34

GUNVOR PARKED her car in the small parking lot just outside Fruängen's subway station. She did not want to risk spending hours looking for a parking space in Old Town, so she had decided to take the train instead. The reason she had even gotten the car at all was to be able to quickly drive to Kungens Kurva and buy groceries once her business in town was done. The group was meeting in just a few hours, and even though everyone had been very appreciative and polite about the turrón and liquor the night before, she had sensed that some good sandwiches would have been more satisfying. She had forgotten that Elin and David still had that young people's metabolism. She, herself, had not had a workout in over a month and had adjusted her calorie intake accordingly. Gunvor had always been lean. But that was, in large, thanks to her diet and workout regimen. Problems with her knees forced her to stay fit and light. During her time with Kjell in Gran Canaria, it had seemed like too much of a hassle to start a new gym membership. It had been too hot, and she had felt that she needed some time just to relax after the traumatic last case. Now she felt the repercussions of her slacking. Her knees had not been this bad in years. That made it even harder to start working out again even though she knew she had to at some point, or it would only get worse.

It really was not like her at all to put things off like this. She wondered if age was finally catching up to her. After all, she had already passed sixty and heading toward seventy. The thought made her cringe. It had been a long time since she had a friend her own age. The thought of giving up work and becoming a pensioner, which was probably the most natural thing to do for someone her age, scared her. It felt like giving up. Swimming, that might do it. She would try swimming for a couple of weeks before going back to lifting weights.

There was only a short walk between the subway station at Slussen and Carl Cedergren's office. This time she had called ahead. Carl had asked if it was really necessary to meet rather than to just speak on the phone, and Gunvor had been polite but adamant. With a slight sigh, he agreed to invite her to his office.

Like last time, Gunvor was led straight into the beautiful office without having to wait in the reception area. But she thought she noticed a bothered expression in Carl's sun-tanned face.

"Hello, Gunvor. What can I do for you today? I doubt that I have any information that would be interesting to you but let's hear what you've come up with."

Gunvor had a hard time telling if his tone was condescending or an attempt to sound lighthearted.

"I have a few... how shall I put it..." Gunvor had practiced pretending like she was looking for the right words. "Delicate questions."

She waited to see if there would be a reaction before she continued, but Carl seemed completely indifferent.

"The reason I want to ask you these questions is that it has come to my attention that another person that seems to have been somewhat in Per's vicinity has also gone missing. Under mysterious circumstances."

"Okay, go ahead. I've heard it all before."

"Last time we met, you told me that Per spends quite a lot of his time in bars and nightclubs."

She waited for Carl to confirm before continuing.

"Yes. I think we were a little more explicit than that, but sure."

"Have you ever had any reason to believe that he might be visiting any kind of... specialized bars and nightclubs?"

Carl looked amused.

"Are you talking about strip clubs? It's not anything we've been talking about, but he is a man after all."

"Actually, I'm talking about gay bars."

The smile vanished from Carl's lips.

"What the hell are you trying to tell me?"

Even though Gunvor had not anticipated Carl embracing the possibility of his son being gay with open arms, she had not expected the reaction to be this strong. She cursed herself for not having opened up the discussion with her other question.

"Get out of my office, woman!"

"Wait, hold on. Hold on. I'm not making any suggestions. I'm asking a simple question. I know plenty of people that go to gay bars because they have better drinks." She quietly asked herself why she had not just said that she knew people who went to gay bars because they had gay friends. Which was actually true. But Carl seemed to calm down a little. "I'm not saying that Per is into that stuff—I mean, he's married, right?

But I needed to ask you to make sure he's not acquainted with the other missing man because there have actually been murders surrounding that investigation. I just want to make sure that Per is not in any danger."

Carl let go of her arm.

"He's not one of those. Just so you know."

"I understand, that's what I thought. If you don't mind me saying, he strikes me as quite the opposite. Quite a womanizer, wouldn't you say?"

This comment cheered up Carl considerably, and he seemed almost jolly as he continued the conversation.

"That's what I've been saying! He gets it from his father. But anyway, what is all this talk about murder?"

"A colleague of mine is working on another case, where an acquaintance of the missing person has turned up dead. The police don't seem to have any strong leads. Although the link between the victim and the missing person doesn't seem very significant and might not be of interest to our investigation at all, when something this serious happens, we want to make sure that we've covered our bases."

Gunvor paused to figure out how to go about her next question. There was a real possibility that Carl would get angry again and throw her out of the office this time.

"My next question might also seem provoking. Let me just say that, like the first question, this is not about making assumptions about Per. There are just details surrounding the case that forces me to ask. May I ask you the question?"

He nodded.

"Do you know if Per has been using any illegal substances?"

Carl scratched his head. To her surprise, he did not seem offended by the question.

"I don't know what to tell you. I really wouldn't know. That's not something he would ever speak about with me. I know that there are a lot of party drugs out there, and I know that Per likes to party, but that's it."

Gunvor was satisfied with the answer. That seemed about as close to a confirmation as she would ever get out of Carl. She thought it was probably best to thank him and excuse herself while he was still in good spirits.

"How is the search coming along anyway? It seems a bit scattered if you don't mind me saying?"

He held on to the hand that she had offered for a handshake in a firm grip.

"Honestly? I think he'll return when it suits him. Probably when his two weeks of leave from work are up. It seems that this is a domestic issue, and his wife hasn't exactly been cooperative. With a case like this, we can't do things like pulling cell phone and GPS-data to track him, so I would be surprised if we managed to find him before he comes back on his own. But since I've been tasked with finding him, I will do my very best with the means available."

"I understand. Well, good luck."

Minutes later, she was walking back towards Slussen in the cold November rain. In hindsight, she was proud of how she had been able to handle Carl's sudden outburst. He certainly did not strike her as someone you wanted as an enemy. Probably not someone you would want to be raised by either. But Gunvor, who had been raised in a very strict family herself, knew that a strict upbringing could take you far in life. At least far as careers go.

CHAPTER 35

GUNVOR'S IDEA of preparing sandwiches proved to be a success. She had put cheese, roast beef, and vegetables on rustic baguettes in a few different combinations and served them, together with fresh fruit, on a large tray. None of the others had eaten since breakfast, and they were all thankful for getting something more substantial than nougat in them before the meeting started.

"Wow, you should start a café when you get tired of the detective business." David took a big bite out of his sandwich before he seated himself.

Gunvor was the only one who had been fully updated on the progress made since their last meeting. Everyone else was waiting eagerly to share their stories and hear what the others had been up to. Elin started by telling the group about Thomas' new information, that Per was likely using drugs. When Aidan told the group about his disappointing phone call with Marie, who was not at all interested in any collaboration, the mood around the table darkened considerably. It did not help that both Eva and Carl had been reluctant to answer any questions, although it was a slight relief that Carl had admitted the possibility that Per might be using drugs.

What really got the discussion going, though, was David's breakthrough. That Per also seemed to be friends with John Doe. That meant there was a tangible possibility that he also knew Seb. The fact that there was now a common denominator between the cases felt like the biggest discovery in the investigation so far. However, it was not entirely clear what the discovery meant. They all agreed that it did not necessarily mean that Per was gay. He could very well just be a friend of John Doe, and possibly Seb. The drug lead seemed somewhat promising and could explain why John Doe had been so cryptic in his conversation with Aidan. And while Aidan did not have any reason to believe that Seb was involved with drugs, Thomas's account of the drug scene within the community had to be taken into the equation. Maybe the three of them—John Doe, Per, and Seb were in the drug trade, and somehow that had prompted them all to disappear from the scene for a while. The weakness of the theory was, as Elin pointed out, that Per was already the heir of a very successful business. Why would he take the risk of getting involved in this?

Since Marie had been very clear that she did not want anyone other than Aidan helping her with the investigation, they decided to stage a little coup. They were all in agreement that finding out if Hampus would recognize Seb as a friend of Per was the next step of the investigation.

CHAPTER 36

AIDAN DID NOT KNOW where he was supposed to meet up with Marie. On their call the night before, she had just asked him to come out with her. Having grown increasingly tired of her mood swings and stubbornness, he had avoided texting her to ask about it or come up with suggestions. He had other things to do anyway, like catching up with the work for which he actually got paid. It was time she took the reins for once. After all, it was her friend, not his, that was missing. If she did not want the help that Gunvor had offered, she could at least make a little effort herself to move the investigation forward. Not just count on Aidan to do everything. He did his best not to think about her all day without much success. At least he did not call her.

In the late afternoon, his phone finally buzzed with a text from Marie, asking if he wanted to meet her at Slussen around 7 p.m. He replied with a short "okay." Nothing more. It served her right to get a little taste of her own medicine. Although, he wondered whether she would even notice.

CHAPTER 37

DAVID FELT EXTREMELY uneasy as he walked the few blocks between his own home and the building he had seen Hampus enter earlier. It had taken less than a minute of online searching to confirm that a Hampus Lindén lived at the address. David was surprised how smooth that part of the mission had been. However, this part, knocking on Hampus' door, telling him that he had been following him home and then asking him for more help, was something David did not look forward to at all. Maybe Hampus would think David had a thing for him. He had to be very clear that was not the case. At the same time, he had to be friendly. After all, they needed his help, and it was up to David to make sure they got it.

Elin had agreed to meet them by the subway station and go with them into the city. David felt like he needed her to give the investigation credibility, making it seem serious to Hampus and buffer for the awkwardness between them. But all of that would only be relevant if David managed to get Hampus to come with him.

There was a code lock on the front door. Luckily for

David, the postal service had, at some point in history, demanded that an area code was added to the locks as an extra alternative to the house code to make life easier for the postal workers. Of course, that area code had leaked long ago and had been common knowledge to every youth in Fruängen for as long as he could remember. Walking up the narrow staircase, David was overcome with a feeling that reminded him of going to the dentist. The same sense of ever-growing terror that just got worse and worse, the closer you got to the appointment and the knowledge that no one would be sympathetic or understanding if he backed out of it.

As soon as he rang the doorbell, he heard steps from the apartment's inside, glimpsing a shadow behind the door eye. When the door finally opened, Hampus, partly to David's relief, gave him a suspicious frown rather than a happy smile.

"Hi. Sorry to bother you. As I mentioned yesterday, I'm a part of a team looking for some missing people."

He paused to make sure that Hampus followed and was not going to demand an explanation of how he had found his address. Hampus shrugged.

"Would you be willing to have a look at one more photo? It's of the other missing person, and since you recognized the first one, Per, it would help us out if you could see if you recognize this guy."

"Alright, sure. Let me see the picture."

"Oh, great. There's just one little problem. I don't have it, strictly speaking. The person who has reported him missing refuses to give out the photo.

CHAPTER 38

IT WAS FREEZING on the subway platform. Elin had chosen fashion over comfort, as was her newly acquired habit. She could have waited inside, by the ticket office, but David's old friends were there, making a racket. Not that they would be bothering her, now that their ringleader, David, was missing. But they were still loud and annoying.

She was excited. It was Wednesday evening, and she had no idea what twists and turns the night might take. She had told Thomas that she would be meeting him at Urban Deli later in the evening. He had given her his number so that she could text him if she got caught up in the investigation.

Actually, that was not the real reason he had given her his number. They had agreed to stay in touch. Thomas wanted to invite her over for dinner. He had told her he had a risotto recipe that she positively had to try.

When David and Hampus appeared at the far end of the parking lot, she suddenly realized what was about to happen. She rushed through the ticket office, through the gates, and out to the parking lot.

David looked surprised as she came rushing towards them with quick steps. She made an effort to look friendly and accommodating as she smiled towards Hampus and offered a handshake.

"Elin."

David, who was very puzzled by this sudden interaction, started to explain.

"This is Elin, my colleague. She…"

Elin interrupted him.

"I'll explain. You go ahead. We'll meet you on the train, first car."

"But…"

"Go."

David gave her a confused look but obeyed and started walking towards the station. Elin turned to Hampus.

"Sorry about that. The thing is, David was or is maybe, I don't know, part of Fruängen's knucklehead gang. You know the ones that hang out by the station and on the high street corners trying to pick a fight with anyone who's not exactly like them. They're all in the ticket office, and if we all came in there together, it would just turn into a big scene, which I don't think anyone would enjoy. I like David and all, but he is kind of like a douchebag moonlighting as a good guy."

"Oh, so that's where I knew him from." Hampus smiled knowingly. "So, he's like a 'dirty cop' then? Aren't those guys up to all kinds of illegal stuff?"

"I know." Elin rolled her eyes. "But he is, kind of, on the right path now. He's not so bad once you get to know him."

Hampus shrugged.

"Listen, you should know that we're all very grateful for your help. We're very aware that you have no obligation towards us. Thank you. Shall we?"

Elin hooked on to Hampus arm, hoping she had convinced him. When she started walking towards the subway, he followed her across the parking lot. When they reached the ticket office, chatting about the cold weather, no one seemed to notice them. David was talking to three other young men by the ticket barriers.

"Gotta go, guys."

They heard David's voice just as they got out on the platform, but they had already gone all the way to the first train car, at the far end of the platform, and seated themselves before David caught up to them. His eyes flickered with paranoia in all directions.

"Sorry." He looked at Hampus, then out the window, as the train left the station. He was ashamed that he lacked the courage to stand up for himself, which in turn put Elin and Hampus in a degrading position. At the same time, it was hard to break free from his old gang. They had been his whole world for so many years. His childhood friends. And it was not like they were evil or even necessarily inconsiderate people. They had just all been brought up with a certain outlook on the world. A view that now seemed to ring less true to David for each day that passed.

Hampus sighed.

"I'm used to it. It's bullshit, but I'm used to it."

CHAPTER 39

THE ORIGINAL IDEA had been for Gunvor to show up at the spot Aidan was meeting Marie as if she just happened to walk past them on her way to somewhere else. Then they could strike up a conversation, and Gunvor could introduce herself and gently convince Marie to collaborate with them. But Aidan had objected to the plan. Knowing Marie, he felt it was too high of a risk that she would see through their little act. A betrayal like that would, no doubt, be enough for her to break all ties to him.

The disappointment of being so far removed from the action made Gunvor restless and put her in a dark mood. Being a control freak was just a part of it. More importantly, she thrived on being in the eye of the storm. She was grateful for all the help she was getting and was well aware that she would not have made it far without her team. They all deserved a chance to shine. But she envied them for the excitement she would now be missing—a chance to really feel alive.

Instead of just sitting around and dwelling, she decided to

try Felix's apartment again. Maybe he would be home by now. And if not, it would at least give her something to occupy her mind for a bit.

CHAPTER 40

MARIE WAS chatty and in high spirits, in stark contrast to her usual mood when they met up. She suggested that they grab a beer at Oliver Twist to plan the night, and Aidan agreed, despite having prepared his own plan. Marie suddenly seemed like a totally different and much more pleasant person. Aidan wondered to himself if he had been too intrusive and dominating until now. Had he made her close herself off, or was it maybe that it just took this long for her to get comfortable with another person?

The venue was full, as usual. The happy hour was long over, but the guests were still sticking around, having a good time. It took Aidan some effort to force his way to the bar and order a London Porter and a glass of the house white. As an avid beer lover, he had been getting increasingly tired of the nondescript lagers that were on tap in most of the nightclubs they had been frequenting lately. So, it was not without some satisfaction that he poured the porter into a glass that had evidently come straight from the dishwasher and was still a bit too hot. He glanced down at his wristwatch as he raised his glass. It was time to start putting his plan into action.

"So." He paused. "Did you have anything particular in mind for tonight?"

"Not really, I just thought—it's Wednesday, a lot of people are out and about. Might be a good night to look for him, don't you think? Do you know any other places than those we've already been to, or should we just try Patricia again?"

Aidan shuddered when she brought up Patricia. He was still shaken up over the murders. But since Marie had seemed neither sympathetic nor interested last time he brought it up, he kept it to himself.

"I actually remembered something today. There's a place Drew always goes on about, but I've never been there myself. It's just by Mariatorget, so it's not far from here. We could give it a go if you want to?" He tried acting as casual as possible, but he wasn't much of an actor, and he could feel the blood rushing to his head as he heard how strange his voice sounded all of a sudden. "I mean, we could just drop by and see what it's like if you want to. If it's dead, we could just go to Patricia. Or we could go straight to Patricia. It's all the same to me." He looked at his watch again, despite having just checked the time thirty seconds ago. "Maybe it's too early anyway. What do you think?"

"Uhm, sure. We can check it out. I don't mind. Let's do that first and take it from there."

Aidan didn't think Marie seemed too suspicious. The plan had been to plant the idea of the new bar subtly so she would think of it as her decision to go there. He excused himself and asked her to keep an eye on his beer while he went to the toilet. When he had locked the door, he picked up the phone and typed a message.

"At Oliver Twist, but we'll head to Side Track in about one beer. Try and get there ahead of us if you can."

After he sent the text, Aidan made sure to both flush the toilet and run the tap. It was essential not to leave any gaps in the plan's execution, even if the chance of Marie being able to hear, let alone take any notice of whether or not someone flushed in the gentlemen's bathroom stall was very slim.

When he came back, Marie did not seem the least suspicious. She told him about some movie she had seen the night before and was excited about it. It was very unusual to see her in such good humor. Aidan was happy that she seemed to be doing well. But he could not help but wonder if it might be, at least to some degree, an act. It did not take long before he got his answer.

"I'm sorry things got a bit heated when we spoke on the phone."

She stared at the floor as she spoke. Aidan thought she looked like a child, forced to apologize by a parent. He wondered if her strained attitude was a result of true regret or just an unwillingness to apologize. But as she looked up again, there was an undeniable sincerity in her eyes.

"I know that you're just trying to help me, and I am grateful for that. Truly. It's just that Seb is kind of a private person, and I know he wouldn't appreciate me dragging other people into this. If it turns out he comes back with some natural explanation, I don't want to come across as hysterical and importunate, having fired up a full-blown investigation."

After looking up at Aidan's confused face, she seemed to want to explain herself further.

"Don't get me wrong, I'm still worried, really worried. But I don't know everything about him. He's done stupid things in the past. I just thought he may have grown up."

"But do you still want to look for him?"

"Yes! Yes, I want to do what I can to find him. But without violating his privacy. Does that make sense?" She didn't wait for Aidan to reply before she continued. "After all, he's part of a pretty shady scene. I don't want more people than necessary to find out."

Aidan had to contain himself not to scoff. Shady scene? He wondered what Seb even saw in her. Surely those eyes couldn't have the same effect on him.

CHAPTER 41

ELIN TRIED her best to improve the mood of their little group, and after a while, she finally managed to get David and Hampus to loosen up a little. In a way, she could understand both of them. They were so different from each other that the mere appearance of the other man might be seen as a provocation to each of them. Especially seeing as they were both young people struggling with their identities. She was very aware of David's situation. It had only been a few months since their first encounter when he and his friends had harassed her. In that short time, he had made a remarkable transformation towards becoming a thoughtful and generous person. Even though he was still sometimes prone to live by his old preconceptions and prejudice, he was clearly a changed person. Their friendship was evidence of that. Therefore, she was willing to help him save face in situations like these, in front of his old friends, knowing that she one day soon would not have to.

She did not know Hampus, but she felt like she had picked up enough from her conversations with Thomas to guess that he might have had to struggle for the acceptance and respect from his surroundings. They were of different generations, but even though times had changed, there was always prejudice.

The train was approaching Zinkensdamms subway station when David got a text from Aidan.

"It seems like he has done it. They're heading to Side Track soon."

"Great. Have you explained everything to Hampus?"

"Yes."

Hampus and David answered at the same time. Hampus continued.

"But David, you really need to be a little more convincing tonight."

David did not get the comment initially, but when Hampus and Elin both burst into laughter, he did his best to look amused, even though he felt quite the opposite.

"Poor David." Elin patted his knee. "Just don't get too mixed up with your character, like I did last time. It's a dangerous game."

"I guess you can play my slow cousin or something. Elin, you get to be my dyke friend." Hampus smiled.

"Fine by me."

"No, but seriously, I know a lot of people at SideTrack. I need to be able to explain why I come dragging with you two. I guess someone might have seen me talking to David yesterday, but no one asked about it, so we're free to come up with anything. Okay, how about this. We all met at a summer course for dance improvisation. Somewhere out of town, maybe Skurup, that's way down south. My parents are from there, and they have a college."

David was happy with any story that did not include him being gay.

"Sounds good. Just remember that I injured my foot during dance practice last week. So, no dancing for me tonight, unfortunately.

Hampus and Elin laughed. The mood had changed considerably since they left Fruängen. When they got off the subway at Mariatorget, they already looked convincingly like the three good friends they were supposed to be.

CHAPTER 42

GUNVOR once again parked her car outside the apartment building, where Felix lived on Reimersholme. It had been dark outside for a while, and the night was cold and windy. She tried the front door even though she knew it would be locked. She would have to wait outside for one of the building's residents to enter or exit so that she could hopefully sneak in like last time. Luckily, she was dressed for the occasions in warm winter clothes.

After what seemed like a long while, a teenage girl finally walked out the door.

"Hello, dear."

"Hi."

The girl held the door. She seemed utterly oblivious to the fact that Gunvor was a stranger. Gunvor wondered if she could not tell her apart from the other older women living in the building or if she just did not care.

Like last time, there was no sign of Felix. When Gunvor peeked through the maildrop, using the flashlight on her phone, there was the big stack of flyers, papers, and envelopes on the floor of the dark hallway. Much more than last time. Either Felix was a real slob or had not been home for at least a few days. Gunvor wondered where he could be. It was a bit strange that he had not called Urban Deli if he had planned on going away. On the other hand, he was a young man and likely a drug dealer. He might not be constrained by conventional etiquette. Besides, he did not really have any obligations towards Urban Deli, just being someone they called from time to time when they were short-staffed. With a job like that, you could not even be guaranteed to make rent. Maybe he had just given up on the restaurant job and gone away on a trip with his friends or something.

Gunvor sighed deeply. She remained by the door for a while, thinking over her options. Maybe someone at the agency could help her track Felix's parents or siblings—she felt conflicted about it. It would be good to talk to him and, if nothing else, to scratch him off the list. But she was not sure if his connection to Per was strong enough to warrant bringing his family into it. If Felix was just providing him drugs, and Per was away with some woman, he was not likely to have any useful information for her. She decided that the best alternative, for now, was probably also the least satisfying—waiting.

CHAPTER 43

AIDAN SAW DAVID, Elin, and their new companion as soon as he and Marie walked through the doors of Side Track. The music was already getting loud, and the venue started to fill up, but it was still possible to have a more or less normal conversation. He let Marie lead the way, and luckily they ended up right next to the others once they had ordered their drinks at the bar. He could not help but admire his young friends' level of professionalism. They did not convey, in any way, that they knew Aidan. They were talking and laughing amongst themselves and seemed just like any other party in the club. Aidan had to remind himself not to stare at them. There was nothing weird about him looking around the venue. He was supposed to do that. Keep his eyes out. But it was hard to look at his friends just the right amount. If he stared at them or avoided them, Marie could get suspicious.

When he asked Marie who they should talk to first, she pointed to a man who had been standing by himself, leaning on the bar. The man did not recognize Seb, and explained, at length, that he was from out of town, Västerås, and this was his first time visiting Side Track. He was very excited about his visit and about the city's general acceptance of all sorts, as he phrased it. Aidan felt a little bad for trying to end the conversation so quickly. However, that did not seem to register with the man, who kept up a monologue, leaving no room for Aidan to excuse himself. Finally, Marie came up and tugged at Aidan's arm. The man noticed and raised his glass in a farewell as he disappeared into the crowd.

Marie rolled her eyes and smiled.

"I better keep my eyes on you tonight."

At that moment, Elin passed them on her way to the bar. She smiled faintly at Marie when their eyes met.

"I guess I could say the same to you," Aidan replied jokingly.

Marie did not seem to have heard him. She had turned around and was now approaching Elin at the bar. They were just a few meters away, but there was enough noise in the club that Aidan could not overhear their conversation. Marie picked up her phone, and Aidan guessed she must have shown Elin the picture. She was not wasting any time. Elin shook her head without even looking at the phone and then said something and pointed towards David and Hampus.

When Elin had gotten her order from the bar, Marie followed her back to the table where David and Hampus were seated. Aidan walked up to the table just in time to hear Elin pretend to explain the situation to her friends.

"She's looking for her friend that has gone missing. I told her I'm rarely in Stockholm but that you live here. Hampus, do you know this guy?"

Hampus looked at the picture and nodded.

"Yeah, I've seen him around. He's usually here with

another guy about the same age. I've seen them here and at Patricia, but it's been a while now."

"What about his friend? Is he here tonight?"

Hampus looked around the room. "I don't think so, sorry."

Marie turned to Aidan with a hint of a smile.

"At least it's something."

Then she suddenly turned back to Hampus again.

"Have you been with him?"

Aidan was both surprised and very uncomfortable with the question. Despite having spent many years in Stockholm, he still found it hard to get over the Swedes straightforwardness sometimes.

"What? Your friend? Eh, no?" Hampus giggled.

When he saw Marie's puzzled expression, he continued.

"Are you serious? He's ancient!"

CHAPTER 44

ELIN, Hampus, and David had decided to stick around at Side Track as long as Marie and Aidan were there, to make sure their meeting did not seem like a setup. At first, it had been a little strange. They had to more or less stay in character in case Marie should overhear their conversation. But at the end of the night, they had almost forgotten that they were there for work. Even David was feeling quite comfortable now that Elin was around, and Hampus had gotten bored of teasing him. When they finally started their journey back to Fruängen, they had all had their fair share to drink, and they really felt like they were all good friends.

On the subway, Elin made a short story long when telling Hampus about her relationship with her ex, Chibbe, for most of the ride home. When they arrived in Fruängen, David walked a bit behind Elin and Hampus just in case his old friends would still be hanging out around the ticket office. But the whole train station was empty, and he caught up with them again just outside the drugstore by the parking lot.

Hampus was struggling with the zipper on his jacket that he had left open on the train ride.

"It's been a great night, guys. So exciting. It was like an undercover investigation. There is just one thing I really don't understand."

"What's that?" David was proud of what little experience he had accumulated and was eager to help explain.

"Why did you need me to look at that photo again?"

"What do you mean—again?"

David and Elin both stopped in their tracks and stared at Hampus.

"I mean, I've already told you I recognize him."

Hampus inspected David and Elin, who both looked like time had stopped.

"The missing guy in the photo? Per? You showed me the same picture yesterday, remember?"

CHAPTER 45

AIDAN AND MARIE were on their way to Patricia when he felt the phone vibrating in his pocket. He did not want Marie to catch a glimpse of the text, in case it was from David, Elin, or Gunvor, so he ignored it for the time being. It felt important not to get Marie suspicious in any way. His head was already a mess from having to pretend that he did not know the guys at Side Track and constantly watching his tongue as not to say anything incriminating. It was especially hard after a few beers. He decided to get mineral water as soon as they got to Patricia and to check the text message on his phone as soon as he got the chance.

It took a while before Aidan had a moment alone. Marie had gone to the bar to get them drinks, but it had felt too risky picking up the phone—what if she should turn around. She ignored his requests for mineral water. She said it would seem suspicious to drink water in a bar. Typical plainclothes, she said. Aidan did not quite understand what was so wrong about that. She would not hear his arguments about how the younger generation chose to abstain from alcohol to a much higher degree.

"I'm sure your new healthy life-style can wait until tomorrow. Just take the beer and stop acting so strange."

She handed him both drinks and excused herself to use the restroom. Aidan found an empty spot at the bar to put down the drinks and got the phone out of his pocket. The text from David did not make any sense. It was impossible. And on top of that, there was no way he could tell Marie about it without revealing that he knew David and Elin. She would never talk to him again. Not that he cared that much about staying friends with her any longer. But if David's text was correct, she would be vital to the investigation.

There was no way he would mess up the case. He just had to keep his head cool for now and discuss the next move with the rest of the group. If Seb and Per really were the same person, there was no telling what kind of rabbit hole they were heading down.

CHAPTER 46

IT WAS WAY past midnight when Aidan knocked on Gunvor's door. David and Elin were already there. Once he realized that it would be impossible to act casual in front of Marie with the news about Per and Seb floating around his head, he had told her that an important meeting had suddenly been moved up to early next morning. He had to go home to prepare and get some sleep. She had accepted the explanation without much fuss.

Gunvor had prepared a pot of strong coffee for Aidan. She suspected that Hollywood films had somewhat exaggerated the sobering effects of coffee over the years, but at least it could not hurt.

"This is insane! Are you sure it's the same guy? Why would he go by two names? What is he, a spy?"

Aidan finally got to ventilate the feelings that had bubbled up inside him since he got the news.

"Actually, I don't think it's two different names. It's just his actual name and a nickname, based on his last name. He knew Marie from high school, right? Well, maybe there was already another Per in his class." David looked delighted to be the first one to have gotten it.

"Oh, of course." Gunvor got excited as well. "Cedergren - Seb."

"Shouldn't it be Ced? I guess that wouldn't really roll off the tongue. Good job, David" Elin patted David on the shoulder.

"Okay. That makes sense, I suppose. But still. He must have been living some kind of double life. Marie certainly doesn't seem to know that he is married." Aidan scratched his head. "More of a triple life, really. One with his wife, one with Marie, and one on the club scene."

"So, all these things we've heard about Seb, it's been Eva's husband all along. I have a suspicion she's not going to be thrilled to hear about it." Elin wondered to herself how you could live with someone without noticing that they had a completely different life on the side.

"And Marie. She couldn't have talked to anyone at his workplace like she said she did. I'm starting to wonder how well they knew each other." Aidan looked pensive.

"It was probably just something she made up. She said she didn't want to come off as importunate, right? And she must have realized that if she told you the truth about not having contacted his workplace, you wouldn't let it go." Gunvor chimed in.

"Could be." Aidan nodded thoughtfully. "The question now is, how do I let her know that her friend has been married all along without telling her? And how do I explain that I know about it?"

"You could just tell her I showed you the picture of Per. After all, it is remarkably negligent of me not to have done that already. We could have figured this out days ago." Gunvor had been cursing herself for her stupidity ever since she got the text from David. "But I don't understand how the man has pulled off living parallel lives like this. And another thing that really stands out as weird to me is his relationship with Marie. He is married to a woman, right? He lives it up at the gay bars during the nights. That is a bit controversial, sure, but not unheard of, so why does he need Marie? It would be one thing if she were his closest friend and confidante that stuck with him through everything, but she doesn't seem to know the first thing about him? If they have known each other since they were kids, how could he possibly have been able to hide the fact that he has a wife?"

"Maybe he's a calculating bastard who just keeps her as company if in case he should be seen by someone. So that they'd think he's a womanizer and not a...manizer?" David, who had been quiet for a while, entered the speculations.

"It's a thought, but she seems like a bad choice for that since she doesn't even enjoy going out, and she also seems pretty homophobic," Elin replied.

"So, what do you think? Do I tell Marie or not? I think she deserves to know, but there's definitely a risk that I won't be seeing her again if I tell her. Do we need her?"

"It's a tough call. I have the same feelings about Eva. If I call her with this story, I'm pretty sure she'll fire me. On the other hand, she is paying me to find him, and at this point, I'm extremely curious to see where this all leads. What do you think?" Gunvor looked to Elin and David.

"Hell, if I know..." David's head was spinning from everything that was going on.

"I don't know either. Why don't we sleep on it? If we get some rest and sober up properly, maybe this bomb will be easier to defuse in the morning. We should think of every possible consequence before we make our next move. I don't want to risk missing anything because we're too tired. I suggest I skip school tomorrow, and we'll all meet up here again at 10 a.m."

"But you can't skip…" Gunvor began.

"Oh, give it a rest. Is 10 a.m. good for everyone?" Elin cut Gunvor off with a determination she had never shown before.

The others nodded in agreement, and thus, the meeting was concluded.

CHAPTER 47
THURSDAY, NOVEMBER 5

AT 10 A.M. SHARP, everyone had taken their seats around Gunvor's kitchen table once again. Gunvor acknowledged to herself that these were some of her favorite moments. Having everyone gathered in her kitchen so that she could treat them to something nice while unraveling a mystery together. The discussion was much like the night before. Everyone had a hard time wrapping their heads around the idea that Per and Seb were one and the same.

"Telling the women would be too risky. They are both too likely to get upset and cut all ties with us, and we might still need information from them. We need to focus on finding the one person that really seems to know Per or Seb or whatever his name is - John Doe. He's the key." David looked at Aidan, who was the only one of them who had met John Doe.

"How about we go to Patricia tonight? All of us? We all know what he looks like. Thanks to you, Aidan."

Aidan was happy to get credit from Gunvor, even though he did not quite agree on the plan.

"It was pretty meaningless to go there last night, and I

think it would be the same thing tonight. As I understand it, he usually only goes there on Sundays. We would probably have a better shot at Side Track, or maybe Urban Deli. Elin, have you shown Thomas the photo of John Doe? If not, it would be good to see if he recognizes him."

"Yes, that's a good point. Gunvor, why don't you come with me to Urban Deli, and you two go to Side Track."

"Sounds like a plan."

"I'm just thinking about what you said, David, about not mentioning anything to Eva or Marie. I agree that we shouldn't say too much to Eva just yet. But I think maybe I should tell Marie. She's so mysterious and closed off that she's not likely to give us any useful information anyway. Perhaps the shock of the news that Seb's married will get her to open up a little. And it's not like I work for her. If she decides to walk away, it's not the end of the world." Aidan had contemplated this for a while and could not see any other viable options.

Gunvor agreed. "To be crude, she hasn't given us any valuable information at all, at least knowingly. So, we don't really need her."

"Okay, that's settled then. I'll make an appointment and tell her the truth about Seb."

CHAPTER 48

WHEN ELIN and Gunvor arrived at Urban Deli, Thomas was already seated at a table with a large pot of tea and three cups in front of him. When he saw them enter the restaurant, he got up from his seat to shake Gunvor's hand and give Elin a warm hug.

"I took the liberty of ordering some tea. I think both Elin and I need to give our livers some rest. Let me know if I can get you anything else."

"Oh, it smells lovely. I'm driving anyhow, so tea will do just fine, thank you." Gunvor sat down as Thomas poured her a cup.

"So, you're the master detective then? Elin has told me a lot about you. I understand your work together means a lot to her."

Gunvor almost blushed. After having put Elin in such a terrible spot in their last case, and also feeling partly responsible for her excessive drinking, it felt good to know that Elin still regarded her as a positive force in her life.

"She means a great deal to me too, both as a colleague and

as a friend. And I'm grateful to you for having helped us in this investigation. It's very nice to meet you finally. Now, if you don't mind, I have a few questions."

"I am happy to help in any way I can."

Gunvor noticed, as she continued, that Thomas seemed to be in a very good mood.

"I have a couple of pictures I would like to show you. You've already told Elin that you recognize Per Cedergren and the waiter, Felix. But haven't seen either of them here for a while, correct?"

"That is correct."

"Have you ever seen this young man?"

Gunvor took up her phone and showed Thomas the picture Aidan had taken of Alexander dancing at Patricia.

"He looks familiar. Like I've seen him recently. But not here, I don't think. I can't remember where."

Gunvor and Elin glanced over at each other.

"Could it be that you recognize him from the papers? He was murdered this weekend."

It took a few seconds for Thomas to react, but when he did, he looked distraught.

"It's that poor fellow that got killed right where I live! I have a houseboat on Söder Mälarstrand. The police came knocking on the door the other day, asking me if I've seen anything." Thomas lashed out with his hands as he continued. "But I was sleeping like a log. There's always a racket there in the evenings. When I moved in there, it was driving me crazy because it kept me up all night, but now that I've gotten used to it, I'll sleep through anything."

"But you didn't recognize him before you saw him in the paper?"

"No, sorry. Should I have?"

"He was on his way home from a gay night at Patricia. I just thought I should ask since you seem to know a lot of people."

"Ah, Patricia. I don't really go nightclubbing anymore. My wild days are behind me. I let the young folks worry about all that."

"I know what you mean." Gunvor smiled. "How about this one? Do you recognize him?" She pulled up the picture of John Doe. Thomas looked closely at it, and after a while, he nodded thoughtfully.

"Yes. Him, I recognize. Seeing him actually makes me remember something." He turned his eyes to Elin. "I know I told you that Per usually comes here alone."

Elin nodded.

"Looking at this picture, something just came back to me. I've seen the two of them having dinner here together. I'm sorry I didn't think of it earlier. It's just one of those things, stuff that happens in the periphery that you just barely notice. It's hard to remember."

"That's very understandable. It's great that you remember it now, though. We've had other indications that they know each other, so with your confirmation, he's now our primary lead. If we find him, we'll likely find Per."

"I'll help you keep an eye out here if you want to. I'm practically part of the furniture here anyway."

Gunvor and Elin giggled at Thomas's comment.

"And you, my dear, need to focus on your future. You should go home and get some sleep for once." He patted Elin on her arm.

"Thank you, that would be really nice, now that you mention it."

CHAPTER 49

NOW THAT SHE was sitting there, across from him at the corner table with a cup of coffee in front of her, Aidan was starting to doubt his decision. The night before, he had been so convinced that he was done with Marie and that he would have no problem with her disappearing from his life. But now, when it was only a few words away from becoming a reality, it all felt different. Even though Marie was far from the kindest and most easy-going person he had ever met, Aidan, for some reason, did not feel ready to let her go. Not yet.

At the same time, he could not possibly go on as though nothing had happened. He had to tell her. In part, because he wanted to see if maybe she would share some information that might be of value to the investigation, in the light of the news. But mainly because it would be a betrayal to keep the information from her. He could not be that cynical. After all, Aidan was her only friend in this whole mess, and she deserved to know the truth about Seb.

Perhaps she would not run away. In that case, he could, in

time and part, replace the friendship she was now about to lose. He had a hard time believing Marie would ever forgive Seb.

"I need to talk to you about something. We just got some new information about Seb."

"We?"

"I was at Gunvor's the other night. She asked me to look at some picture from her investigation. Apparently, the person she's looking for is also part of the gay club scene. So, since I'm already out there pretty much every night, she asked me to keep an eye out."

Marie stayed quiet. She looked at him with an expression he could not quite figure out. Aidan gathered up the courage to put his hand on top of hers before he continued.

"The thing is... I don't know how to put it, so I'll just say it. The photo she showed me was a photo of Seb. She is looking for the same person. Only, she knows him as Per Cedergren."

Marie just stared at him without moving a muscle.

"And the one who had reported him missing and employed Gunvor is his wife. He's married, Marie. I'm sorry. He's been married for many, many years. I don't know how he has managed to keep it secret from you. Or why. But now I've told you the truth."

Marie turned her head and looked out over the town square outside the window. It was only a few days since the first time they sat here at Café Rival, and Aidan had offered to help her find her friend and tried figuring out the best way to go about it. It felt like an eternity ago. The moment was over in a second. Marie stood up and stormed out on the street. Aidan was not surprised—just resigned. He called after her, but only once. He did not try to run after her. It would have been futile anyway, and he did not want to cause even more of a scene. He was already getting judging looks by the other guests. It must have looked like a dramatic breakup. In a way, it was.

CHAPTER 50

EVEN THOUGH IT WAS A THURSDAY, with the weekend coming up, Side Track was unusually quiet. After checking in with Gunvor, David and Hampus decided to call it a night at around 10 p.m. and take the subway back to Fruängen. They had not seen any sign of John Doe. Hampus had done his best to recall any more details about him and Per Cedergren, without much success.

"I mean, I'm going to Side Track this weekend anyway. You don't have to come along if you don't feel comfortable. I'll keep my eyes open and text you if I see him. You could hang out at the bar next door if you want to stay close by, in case he shows up."

David glanced at Hampus to see if he was messing with him again. But he looked sincere.

"Cool. We have to see what Gunvor says. But really, Side Track is not as bad as I first thought. It just... you know things have always been a certain way in Fruängen, and that's what I'm used to. But as a detective, you need to be able to deal with anything, right?"

When he saw the expression on Hampus' face, he quickly tried to correct himself.

"Oh, I didn't mean it like that. It's been cool—people are nice here."

Hampus smiled at David's comment.

"Good to hear." He gave David a friendly pat on the shoulder. "We'll make a man of you one day."

David gave Hampus a mock-offended shove.

"Yeah, you're one to talk."

They were both laughing when the train approached the platform. When the doors opened, Hampus waited to give David a head start past the ticket office, but as soon as David noticed, he turned around and waved at him.

"Hey, man. Keep up!"

CHAPTER 51

IT WAS STILL early in the evening when Aidan knocked on Gunvor's door. They departed from their habit of opening a bottle of wine by making a pot of green jasmine tea. With all that was going on, they enjoyed finally having a moment to relax a little, just the two of them. They both loved having everyone gathered like a big family, but it was also nice to have a chance to go over everything at their own pace.

Gunvor did not feel the same pressure to perform and quickly come to conclusions when they were alone. Not that David and Elin had ever been impatient with her. It was more that she felt some sort of responsibility to be a leader to them. With Aidan, it was different, she did not have to think twice about what she said, and it was fine to come up with thoughts and ideas that were completely stupid.

Even though it was expected, Aidan struggled a little bit with how things ended with Marie. It was not likely that he would ever see her again, and in a way, it seemed as if he had failed her. He had wanted to help her. Maybe she would have been better off without him sticking his nose in her business and finding out about Seb's marriage.

Gunvor told him about the meeting with Thomas and how he and Elin had taken to each other.

"It's a tough age for anyone, and I don't think she's had someone that she feels understands her. And I guess his life has been a little empty as well, and he's happy to have found someone he could mentor. It sounds cynical when I say it like that, but you know what I mean."

She looked at Aidan, who nodded as he was taking a sip of his tea.

"That's how humans work, I suppose. We're hard-wired to strive for love, safety, adventure, the feeling of belonging, feelings of accomplishment, and so on, and so on. Even if it doesn't matter in the greater scheme, it's always nice to find something or someone who gives you these feelings. To make you feel whole. If only for a brief moment."

"That's true. Sometimes, many times, the pursuit can drive us to destructive behavior. But I think, in this case, they've both been lucky."

When they had texted David and agreed he and Hampus would call it an early night at Side Track, she invited them both over for tea, but was careful to point out that it was not a mandatory meeting and if they wanted to go home and get some sleep, that was completely fine. Hampus politely declined, but David was happy for the invitation. Aidan offered to pick him up at the station in his car.

He parked by the local fishmongers, Erssons Fisk, a couple of minutes before the train was supposed to arrive. The night was freezing. So far, it had been an unusually cold November. The last few days had been grey with dense clouds, but now the sky was clear. The street lights around the parking lot were out of order, making it possible to see the stars. Aidan could easily point out Orion's belt and Ursa Major. It made him long for the summer. To sit on the balcony and let the hours pass just talking and looking at the stars.

He was still occupied with the stars when the train came rolling in. He wished he knew more of the constellations. As a kid, he had been trying to find his own zodiac sign, the Pisces. He remembered what it had looked like in the book they had, but he had never been able to find it in the sky. He lowered his gaze and saw David and Hampus walking down the platform. They must have been seated in the middle of the train. He smiled at the notion that he made those kinds of observations now. Maybe he had a detective in him after all.

Suddenly something else caught his attention. Among the people walking down from the far end of the platform, he saw something familiar. Someone. Someone who had seen him too. Marie's eyes were now fixed straight forward, but for a split second, their eyes had met. Aidan was sure of it, despite the dim lighting and the distance between them.

A thousand questions popped into his head. What was she doing here? And what had she been up to? It had been hours since she stormed out from Café Rival. Did she live here in Fruängen, or was she just parked here, or was she taking a bus from here? She disappeared into the station house, and for a moment, he considered running after her but decided against it. He had already endured enough drama for one day.

David and Hampus were the only two people to come out of the exit facing the parking lot. That meant Marie was probably on her way down to the town square. After he greeted the boys, his curiosity got the best of him. He peeked down the staircase between the drug store and Supersaver, leading down to the square. No sign of Marie. She must have either gotten onto the pedestrian road or gone to the bus stops.

"What are you doing?" David looked curiously at Aidan.

"Marie was on your train. Did you see her?"

David and Hampus looked confused at each other.

"No?"

"Does she live here?" Hampus walked up next to Aidan and looked down at the square.

"I have no idea, to be honest. I've spent so many days with her now, and she's still a complete mystery."

"I thought I saw her at Side Track earlier. I think she peeked in for just a second."

"Why didn't you tell me?" David sounded almost a little accusatory.

"I don't know, man. It was just for a second. She turned away as soon as she came in. I've only seen her once, so I wasn't sure it was her. I'm still not sure."

"She was probably looking for Seb. I guess she's even more desperate to find him now, to scold him for not telling her about his marriage." Aidan said.

"If it even was her." It annoyed Hampus that Aidan was jumping to conclusions even though he had now repeatedly said he was not sure whether he had actually seen her.

Aidan insisted on giving Hampus a ride home even though he lived just a block away. After that, he dropped off David, who suddenly had become very sleepy.

"Say hello to Gunvor from me."

Aidan waited until the front door had closed behind David before he drove off. For some reason, a feeling of uneasiness had begun eating away at him.

CHAPTER 52
FRIDAY, NOVEMBER 6

GUNVOR WAS STILL in bed when the phone rang. She looked at the caller ID before picking up. It was Manuel, from the agency.

"Gunvor Ström speaking."

"Yes, I know."

"Good morning, Manuel."

"Our client has terminated the investigation." As usual, he was straight to the point. "The husband has returned home. She is paying us the full fee, so she must be happy with your effort anyway. Good job."

"What happened? Where had he been?" Gunvor was relieved that he was not injured or dead, not that she had ever thought he would be, but she really wanted to know what had happened.

"I don't know."

"She refused to tell you?"

"It's not our business now anyway, is it?"

"Well, it would be nice to know if we were on the right track. Seeing as she was so happy with the investigation."

"I did ask her, actually. I wouldn't use the word refuse, but she did avoid the question."

"Hm."

"Sort of like how you've avoided giving me reports on the case all week."

Manuel was right. She had not given him a single update since she took the case. He did not know anything about any murders or drugs. Gunvor decided to keep it that way. If she told him, he might get protective and keep an extra eye on her to make sure she would not get into any more danger. That would just slow her down.

"Anyway, case closed. If the client is happy, we're happy, right?"

"Right."

"So how are you feeling? Do you need a couple of days to clear your mind, or are you ready to jump on another case if anything develops? We're coping at the moment, but if we get more requests now, we could use some help."

"You know that I prefer to keep occupied. Let me know if anything comes in. And let me know if you hear anything more about Per Cedergren. It would be interesting to know how it all turned out."

"Okay, but I got the sense all was well, probably just a misunderstanding."

"You 'getting a sense' is not the same as facts, and she didn't even tell you anything."

As she spoke the words, Gunvor realized the confrontational tone was neither necessary nor fair. But the thought of leaving the case in an unfinished state with this many loose ends was frustrating.

"Listen, I know you've worked hard on this, and it can be frustrating sometimes to not get proper closure on a case. But it's our job to make the client happy. This client is happy. We can't go around digging in people's private matters just for our own satisfaction."

"But we haven't even talked to Per." Gunvor felt like a defiant teenager, but she could not stop herself.

"Per has never been our client. Let it go."

Manuel sounded tired. Gunvor knew that his discretion and professionalism were pillars of the agency's reputation. However, she felt that her seniority in age should at least grant her some extra freedom in how she conducted her own investigation.

"Okay, Manuel. I'll do my best." Gunvor said before hanging up, even though she was well aware that her best would not be good enough.

CHAPTER 53

FIRST PERIOD WAS ALMOST over when Elin felt the phone vibrating from a text inside her cardigan. She wanted to check it right away, but her teacher was in the middle of a monologue of how they could all improve their essays. As usual, Elin sat in the front row. Even though there was a chance that she might be able to sneak a look at the phone without the teacher noticing, she had too much respect for her. Besides, she was known to make fun of students who were not paying proper attention, and Elin did not want to risk being embarrassed in front of her class.

As soon as the bell rang, Elin rushed out to the corridor and opened the text. It was from Thomas.

Call me as soon as possible!

Elin dialed Thomas's number straight away, worried that something terrible might have happened to him.

" Oh, hi, dear."

She relaxed a little when she heard the soft tone in his voice.

" Hey. Did something happen?"

"Yes, as a matter of fact. I should probably have called you yesterday, but I figured you needed some sleep. I thought it could not possibly be urgent enough to make a fuss in the middle of the night. I hope I wasn't wrong."

"Thomas, please. Just tell me what it is!" Elin was getting worried again.

"Right, of course. I'm sorry. Well, that man you are all looking for—Per's friend. I ran into him yesterday."

"What? John Doe? No kidding? Did you speak to him?"

"Ah, yes, that's what you called him. Yes, we talked for quite a while, actually."

"Did he say anything about Per?"

"Yes, he was the subject of our discussion. Otherwise, I would have been quite a lousy Watson." Thomas chuckled at his own joke for a moment before he continued. "Fact is, he had quite a story to tell. I would like to invite you all over this afternoon when you're all done with your school, and whatever else the rest of them are up to today, so I can give you all the details."

"That sounds great, but I hope you realize you can't leave me hanging like this all day. You need to tell me what happened right now."

"Easy now, easy now, dear. I'll tell you."

Elin glanced up at the big clock in the school corridor.

"Short version, my next period starts in five minutes."

"Very well. He told me that Per had just discovered that he's a father. He has a daughter with another woman. The daughter had looked him up somehow, and one day she just called him up, out of the blue, saying that she wants to meet him. John Doe, as you call him, his real name is Thor, by the way, is Per's best friend. He told me that this was kind of a big shock to Per and that he felt he had to put his ordinary life on hold for a couple of weeks to figure everything out. So basically, he has just been hanging out with his daughter for two weeks."

"Wow, that's about the last thing I would have expected. But good for him."

"Yes, except for the adultery and him taking off for two weeks, leaving his wife worried to death, it's quite a lovely little story."

Other students were now gathering outside the classroom. Hannah, who had been in Elin's class for almost two and a half years but had only recently become a friend, was waving for her to come.

"I'll call you after school. Do you want to call Gunvor? You should do it now. She needs to know this."

Thomas laughed.

"That sounded like a question at first, but I suppose it's an order? Will do, captain."

Elin felt a great relief as she walked over to chat with Hannah. This time the case seemed to have ended on a good note. A long-lost daughter and her father were reunited, and everyone was happy. A perfect ending to all the drama.

CHAPTER 54

GUNVOR WAS as surprised as Elin to hear the truth about Per's disappearance. But she did not share Elin's conviction that this would be the end of the story. There were still too many loose ends. After the conversation with Manuel, she could not possibly call Eva. It would just get back to him, which might make him hesitant to assign her new cases in the future.

When Thomas called and told her about the child, Gunvor immediately thought of her conversation with Annika Rosén. The woman whose daughter, Vera, had gone to visit her father at Nämdö. It could be a coincidence, but it was enough to warrant another call.

It did not take long for Annika to pick up.

"Hello, this is Gunvor Ström. Private investigator. I called you a few days ago."

"Hi, this is about Per, isn't it?"

"So, you do know him?"

"Yes, I suspected he was the one you were looking for. But

I had promised not to tell anyone. I knew he would call his wife soon enough. I hope she hasn't been too worried."

"I honestly don't know." Gunvor felt like she might as well be honest. "This has been a rather strange investigation. I don't know how many of the things we discovered along the way she already knew about. She's been very reluctant to give us any kind of information at all."

"You mean about him having a daughter?" Annika sounded curious.

"Well, there's slightly more to it than that. Would it be okay if I asked you a few questions about Per? I don't mean to be intrusive or get in the way of him and your daughter reconnecting, but it would be helpful."

"Sure, go ahead."

"Supposedly, the reason for his disappearance is that he has been reconnecting with his, and your, daughter. Could you tell me anything about that?"

"Yes. In hindsight, I should probably have told Per when he got me pregnant, but I knew that he was married, and I've been living with another man since Vera was little, so I just thought—why bother him? She's always had a father figure anyway, and I've managed well, so it seemed pointless to complicate things for him. Nevertheless, a while ago, we decided that Vera was old enough to know the truth, so we told her. At first, she was distraught, but pretty soon, she began to get curious. A little too curious for my taste, actually. Two weeks ago, she sent me a text saying she was in Stockholm to meet her biological dad."

"She sounds like quite an ambitious young lady." Gunvor could not help being a little impressed.

"That's one way to put it."

"So, did the meeting go well?"

"Very well. Per drove her back in his car. All the way from Stockholm. He's been living in a hotel here in Sundsvall since then. They've seen each other every day. He's even been to our house for dinner a couple of times, and everyone has been getting along great. It's really been a weight off my chest that it all worked out so well. I never knew Per that well, but now that I've spent some time with him again, I can see where Vera gets a lot of her traits."

"I guess the natural follow up question is, how come you two have a child together in the first place? If you don't mind me asking."

"Oh, well. We actually go way back. We were classmates in high school. I'm originally from Stockholm and didn't move to Sundsvall until I met my husband. Per and I had a short fling back then, but he got together with Eva pretty soon after that."

"So, you know Eva as well?"

"Knew. This was in the mid-'80s, remember. After we graduated, I didn't see either one of them for many, many years. Until my friends and I had a night out in…well, Vera was born in June 2004, so it must have been in the fall of 2003. We were at some night club and started talking to some guys. One of them seemed familiar, so I asked his name. It was Per Cedergren. It was quite late in the evening, and we girls had been having a dinner party at my place with some wine before we headed out, so I was a little tipsy, mildly speaking. I'd always thought Per was really good looking, and he had only improved with age. He said the same thing about me. So, one thing led to another. He was careful to point out that he was married to Eva. But he also said that there was no passion between them."

Gunvor was not sure why Annika was going into such detail, but she thought maybe she never had a chance to tell the story to anyone before, and it was a relief to talk about it with somebody she did not know. Or maybe this was just what she was like.

"I understood then what he was like, or maybe I had already known since high school. He's never been very good with relationships. He has...how should I put it? A thirst for life. It wasn't until now, since I've been talking to him for the last few weeks, that I realized the full scope of it."

"Are you referring to the fact that he's sleeping with both men and women?"

"Sure. I suppose that's why Eva is such a good match for him. According to Per, she lets him do whatever he wants."

"That sounds like an odd relationship." As Gunvor spoke, she thought back on her own failed marriage and thought that maybe this was not that much stranger after all.

"Yes and no. I think you come to realize, more and more with age, that no relationship is a bed of roses."

"You're right. Still, it seems a little sad."

"Yeah. She was always a bit different. Cold, somehow. Hard to grasp. I don't remember her having any female friends. The guys all thought she was hot but stiff."

"Oh, really?" There was something very pleasant about talking to Annika. Gunvor started to feel more and more like she was talking to an old friend rather than gathering information from a witness.

"So, what is it that you've found out? You said that your investigation has been strange? I'm very curious!"

Gunvor could hear in Annika's voice that she was almost as excited as herself.

"Right, so we've followed his tracks to some gay clubs,

which surprised us considering that he's married, but you already knew about that. We've also been led to believe that he's using drugs."

"Drugs, really? I didn't know about that. Frankly, I find it a little hard to believe. Well, what do I know? I better look into that, for Vera's sake. But don't worry, I won't tell him it's coming from you."

"I want to point out that we don't have any hard evidence for drug use, it's just a few stories we heard, and I found a note..." At that moment, Gunvor remembered her own note, the one she had left for Per in the cabin. She hoped no one would get too upset over it. She suddenly felt a stab of self-doubt. Maybe she had been too impulsive. Maybe this was all an intrusion of privacy for the sake of her own curiosity rather than good detective work. She decided to spare Annika the story about the murders. It did not make any sense to worry her with that. But there were still a couple of questions she wanted answered.

"You say Eva lets Per do whatever he wants. The thing is, when I've talked with her, she's been very adamant that Per is suffering from depression and that the disappearance is linked to that. When I asked her about the gay clubs, she almost lost her mind."

"Oh, really? I actually thought that part seemed a bit contradictory when he told me about it. He told me that he's been living a lie for many years. He is bisexual, and Eva doesn't know. Neither does his father. Apparently, the father is an important figure in Per's life, and he is very homophobic. I think the main reason he hasn't told Eva is that he's scared his father might find out. That talk about Eva letting him do whatever he wants, I think what he meant was that she doesn't ask any questions when he comes home late at night or disappears for a day or two from time to time. He's been telling her that he's at dinner meetings and other types of things for the business, and she seems to accept that explanation. So, she's been a convenient partner for him in that sense."

"Okay, that clears things up a bit."

"But this new realization, that he's a father, I think it's changing him. At least he seems to believe so. He's been saying he's ready to become a family man. I don't know about that, but at any rate, Vera is on her way to see them now, to meet Eva."

Suddenly a feeling of uneasiness came over Gunvor.

"Really? Does Eva know about Vera? How did she react to the fact that he has a daughter that is not hers?"

"They haven't met yet. Per and Vera went back to Stockholm yesterday, and he got her a hotel room so that he could tell Eva first in his own time. I just got off the phone with Vera. Per and Eva are on their way to Nämdö right now, and Vera will take the next ferry. I'm not sure why they're not on the same ferry. Maybe Eva needed some time to process everything. Per has quite some explaining to do, I suppose."

Gunvor thought that it seemed like a remarkably bad idea to risk putting a 16-year old between two arguing grown-ups, one whom she had never met and one that she had just recently gotten to know, on an island far off in the archipelago. But she kept that concern to herself.

"Alright, thanks. It's been great talking to you, Annika. If anything else comes up, feel free to call me. The mystery seems to be solved, but you get pretty invested when you're working on cases like this. You just want everything to turn out okay, you know?"

"Of course. It's been good to have someone to talk to about this. I mean, my husband has been great, and he gets along well with Per, but he's not really that excited about listening to me rambling on about someone I had a fling with. Let me know if you're ever in Sundsvall!"

And with that, they ended the call—Annika, seemingly in high spirits, and Gunvor with growing concern.

CHAPTER 55

DAVID WAS as surprised as the rest of the gang to hear the real reason for Per's disappearance. While he was relieved that it had not been anything more menacing, it made Per come off as even more of a prick. Someone who did not have concern for anyone but himself. He thought of his own father, who had abandoned the family just because he felt like it—gone off with a younger woman.

When his father left the family, David had made a vow to himself. Once he met someone he wanted to share his life with, he would never let her down. He would be loyal forever. She would be his everything. The thought of hurting someone the way his father had hurt his mother was so appalling, inhumane. David was aware that he was not always a great guy. He could be obnoxious, mean even. But there was a limit, especially when it came to people who were close to him.

For a while, it had seemed like the investigation would take a much darker turn, and it was probably a good thing that things had turned out the way they did. Still, just because there had not been any violence did not mean people would not get scars. Maybe it would be good for the daughter to get to know her father finally. Maybe it would just be a constant reminder of 16 years of neglect.

Thoughts were flying to and fro in David's mind. He knew that he had siblings. Two younger brothers he had never met. His dad had asked him over, but he had to stand up for his mother. And for himself. Even so, he wondered what it would be like. What they were like. Were they like him? Did they wonder why their big brother didn't want them just like he had wondered why his father hadn't wanted him and his mother?

CHAPTER 56

IT WAS midday when Aidan finally picked up the phone. He had been out for a morning jog and then gone straight to the gym without checking his phone. Working out sometimes felt like the only way he could really clear his mind, and he did not want any distractions. When he opened the locker to get his towel, he peeked at the phone and saw the missed calls from Gunvor. Just as he was going to call her back, it started ringing again.

"Gunvor, are you alright?"

"Yes, sorry if I scared you. I have news. Can you come over?"

He showered and got his clothes on as quickly as he could and then, out of excitement, jogged all the way back home. When he finally knocked at Gunvor's door, he was as sweaty as he had been before he showered. He considered going up to his apartment for another quick shower, but Gunvor had prepared lunch and quickly ushered him to the table.

"This thing gets stranger by the day. We've already

covered infidelity, depression, sexuality, and drug trafficking as possible culprits to the disappearance, and it turns out he's been taking a time-out because he discovered he's a dad."

"You gotta keep your mind open to any possibility in this business and just go where the leads take you. Thank god we got a happy ending this time. And the daughter is a result of an affair, so arguably we weren't completely off the mark even if our timeline wasn't perfect." Gunvor smiled.

"I suppose." Aidan looked deep in thought. "But I still don't get it."

"Get what?" Gunvor knew Aidan well enough to know he easily ran away with his thoughts and could be referring to just about anything.

"Marie. She knows I live in Fruängen. Why hasn't she said anything? I mean, she must have realized that we're bound to bump into each other at some point if she lives here too. She must have gone through some trouble to make sure we never ended up on the same train to the city when we've met up."

"Sometimes, you just can't figure people out. There might be a reasonable explanation, though. Say she changed to a bus here in Fruängen. Maybe she lives in Älvsjö. Then it would normally be more convenient to get the commuter train from Central Station. But if there are severe delays, you could get the subway and then change for the bus in Fruängen."

"I guess you're right."

"Didn't you ever ask her where she lived? Isn't that usually one of the first things that comes up in a conversation with a new acquaintance, or is it just me who's too nosy?"

"I've been curious, but she's particularly good at avoiding questions, and I didn't want to push it. She's a bit unique. Very shy and private. I figured she wanted to take it slow."

"Maybe you could ask her about it when you call to say that Per, or Seb as she calls him, has returned. You are going to tell her, right?"

CHAPTER 57

GUNVOR WAS LOOKING FORWARD to seeing Thomas and the others again. She had bought the nicest boxed wine she could find. She hoped that Thomas would not mind. Many of her generation would consider bringing boxed wine in poor taste. A gay man living on a boat, helping out private investigators in his spare time just for fun, would probably be at least somewhat able to overlook outdated rules of etiquette, she thought. But you could never be sure. Either way, she thought everyone would appreciate a toast for the good work they had put in. It was true they had not solved the case. However, there were other things worth celebrating. Elin and David had really grown into their new roles as investigators and had been able to take fantastic initiatives. Aidan had practically been running his own case. Gunvor was also grateful for the help they had been getting from Thomas and Hampus.

Before she left the apartment, she printed the passenger manifests for the ferries that Helena had sent her and put them in a folder along with all the other notes from the investigation, which she then put in her bag. Manuel had already officially closed the case, but Gunvor wanted to do it her own way and close the books properly, together with her team.

Once she had found a good seat on the subway, she took out her phone to read the news. She had been too busy all day to keep abreast of what was going on outside the investigation bubble. As she scrolled through the news app, she suddenly came across a headline that made her blood freeze. Under the dramatic, bold letters were pictures of a crime scene taken from a drone and a victim's portrait with the caption Felix Wiik.

"Murder victim found on drifting sailboat."

CHAPTER 58

ELIN HAD ALREADY ARRIVED at Thomas's boat when Gunvor texted her to check the news. So, they both got comfortable on the couch with some freshly brewed tea and started scrolling through the news on the laptop. Elin had no idea what it was that Gunvor wanted her to find, if it was good news or bad. If David had been there, they would have laughed, mocking Gunvor for asking them to check the news instead of just sending a link to the article, but she was not sure Thomas would get it. When she finally saw the news, she was shocked. She had assumed it would be something positive.

"What the..." She stared at the bulletin. With a few short sentences, it painted a horrific picture of a sailboat that had been anchored in a curious spot next to a residential area in Saltsjöbaden for two weeks. When the president of the local yacht club had decided to investigate, they walked into a bloodbath. A dead body was found, later identified as Felix Wiik. A young man from Stockholm.

The boat suddenly lurched, which caused both Elin and Thomas to jump. Thomas got up to see what it was, and Elin could hear him greet Aidan and tell him the news about the murder from the deck. When the two men came back down, Aidan fetched his laptop from the bag, and soon all three of them were engulfed in the murder, frantically searching the web for any new information.

CHAPTER 59

DAVID AND HAMPUS had agreed to meet up at Slussen and walk down to Thomas' boat together since neither of them had been there before. When Hampus got off the subway, he saw Gunvor come out of the train car in front of his, and while they waited for David, she updated him on the news about Felix.

Thomas' boat was moored just a short walk from the subway station. Gunvor did not know anything about boats, but she figured this must have been a rather expensive one. It did not have any sails or a mast, so it must be a motorboat, but that was all she could make of it. They jumped on the boat at the stern. There was only a small gap between the quay and the boat, but she gladly accepted David's helping hand because of her problematic knees.

A couple of steps down was a couch and a fixed table which, with some nice cushions, would have made for a wonderful place to have coffee in the summer but looked hard, cold, and uninviting in the brisk November weather. A set of glass doors led into an impressive wheelhouse. Thomas must have felt the boat move as they jumped aboard because he came up to greet them before any of them had a chance to knock on the door. He gave each of them a hug and invited them downstairs.

None of them had ever been on a boat like that before. To the right, just below the stairs, was a small but modern looking kitchenette, and to the left a corner sofa and a fixed table. On the kitchen counter, bottles of spirits stood in a neat row. Many of which Gunvor did not even recognize. He was either traveling a lot or just shopping in a completely different price range than her, she thought. Pots of flourishing herbs accompanied the bottles. Basil, rosemary, and thyme spread a pleasant scent across the lounge.

The beige sofa was not very inviting on its own, but Thomas had done a good job of sprucing it up with cushions and blankets. Elin and Aidan were already cooped up in it. They barely looked up from their laptops when Gunvor, David, and Hampus entered the room.

"Hi there."

At last, Elin and Aidan realized they had more company.

Gunvor turned to Thomas.

" You're the only one of us who knows what Felix from Urban Deli looks like. Is it really him they've found?"

Thomas nodded.

" In all probability, it's the same Felix whose number I found on the note in Per's and Eva's house."

" What is wrong with this world? Why would anyone do something like that to another person? This is such bullshit." Elin sounded more angry than sad.

Thomas politely helped Gunvor with her coat, and after he had taken David and Hampus' jackets, he disappeared into the room next door. Gunvor saw a bed in there and got curious but stopped herself. It was probably more appropriate to save the house tour for another time. When Thomas came back, he had two foldable chairs with him. David and Hampus crowded together with Aidan and Elin on the sofa, and Gunvor took one of the chairs. Thomas made sure everyone got tea and put a tray with large cinnamon buns on the table.

" I must say, I've been a little jealous of your job until now, but this is a bit much, isn't it? Do you think it's the same killer?" Hampus sounded jittery.

" It's impossible to say. We don't really know anything about the murders because we haven't had a reason to look into them. That's police business. Our mission has been to find Per. But now he's back and no thanks to us." Gunvor scratched her forehead." Three murders. Felix must have been the first one, killed on a sailboat. Then Morgan, in the middle of the day as far as we know, in his own apartment. And Alexander killed on his way home from Patricia. They all seem so different."

" Well, there's one common denominator. Morgan and Alexander had both had affairs with Per." Aidan cut in." Maybe Felix did too. At least Per had his number, so they must have had some sort of contact."

" They had one more thing in common." Elin entered the conversation. "At least Morgan and Alexander had met you, Aidan, shortly before they were killed."

"Tell me about it. I've gone over it in my head a million times. But I've never met Felix."

"No, if the timelines are correct, he would have been killed before we even got involved with this." Gunvor paused to think for a moment. "Thomas, do you know if Felix was gay?"

"Sorry, I have no idea. He's way too young for me anyway. We wouldn't run in the same circles."

"I recognize him." Hampus cut in. "I'm not sure where

from, but I've never been to Urban Deli, so it's not from there anyway. I've been trying to remember if it's from any of the gay bars, but I'm really not sure."

"Don't beat yourself up about it. Just the fact that you recognized him is helpful in context. That means we can't write him off as a possible lover to Per." Gunvor said. The room fell silent, with everyone trying to think of something that might be useful.

"Hey, help yourself to some more tea." Thomas said and started refilling everyone's cups himself. "And a cinnamon bun, they're fresh."

"Thank you. I think that's a great idea. They look great. Let's take a short break from the speculations and then we'll go through the whole case bit by bit and see if there's anything more for us to do."

CHAPTER 60

A FEW MINUTES LATER, they were all eager to get back to the case again. Everyone felt a little more at ease after the buns, and to Gunvor's delight, Thomas had shown them around the boat during the break. They had all tried Thomas' hexagonal bed in the front of the boat. The fact that it was dressed in red silk sheets surprised no-one. From the minute they had set foot on board, it had been evident that Thomas was an aesthete with an original taste. At the stern was another room with two guest beds and a cupboard.

"You're welcome to stay here anytime. Maybe we should go on a little cruise in springtime?"

"Yes!"

Everyone liked the sound of that idea, especially Elin, who was delighted to get to visit Thomas in his home finally.

"Shall we get going?" Gunvor was getting a little impatient even though the break had been her idea to begin with.

"I suggest we start at the beginning and see if we can trace Per's footsteps. It all began with him going out to their summer house at Nämdö. While he was there, the daughter came to visit. I managed to get the passenger manifest for all ferries during the period from my nephew's wife. She works at SL."

"Isn't that illegal?" David asked.

Gunvor remembered the promise she had made to Helena, not to spoil the secret, and pretended like she did not hear him. Instead, she picked up the sheets of paper from her bag and waved them in front of everyone.

"I've only checked the ones who left Nämndö on the same ferry as Per on Sunday. It was on that list I found his daughter Vera. Although it took me a while to realize it was his daughter." Gunvor grimaced before she continued. "But I haven't checked when either Per or Vera arrived at Nämdö. Supposedly Per got there the Friday before Vera. It probably won't make a difference either way, but I'd like to have that piece of information confirmed, just to make sure the timeline is correct. Elin and David, would you mind going through the manifests?"

She did not wait for them to answer before handing them the stack of papers. She then turned to Hampus and Thomas.

"Could the two of you make some kind of timeline of when you last saw Per, Alexander, and Felix? I know it's difficult to remember, but it's worth a try. We might find some sort of pattern. And Thomas, do you mind doing this first? We'll get to your conversation with John Doe eventually. Unless there's something you need to tell us right now?"

Thomas shook his head.

"Not really. The big takeaway from that conversation was that Per had been away to be with his daughter. I don't mind doing the timeline first. What do you say, Hampus?"

Hampus nodded.

"So, what am I doing?" Aidan was eager to get an assignment he could sink his teeth into as well.

"Why don't you check the Flashback Forums? I know it's pretty much a troll farm, but I guarantee you someone has posted about this, and if we're lucky, there might be some useful information on there. I will try and make an oversight chart of all the events we know of so far."

For a while, the room was quiet. Aidan scrolled through page after page with offensive remarks about the victim's sexual identity. Thomas and Hampus discussed with muted voices while scribbling down dates on, what looked like, exclusive letter paper Thomas had fetched from a drawer.

"Eva Cedergren went out to Nämdö."

"What do you mean?" Gunvor stared at Elin as if she genuinely did not understand what she was saying.

"Eva took the late Saturday departure to Nämdö. Eva-Marie Cedergren, to be precise."

Everyone looked at Aidan. It took a few seconds for Elin's word to sink in. Once he finally understood the implication, he picked up his phone and found a picture he had taken of Marie at Patricia. He held up the screen in front of Gunvor and saw her jaw drop. In what seemed like slow motion, she lifted a hand to cover up her wide-open mouth.

"What. Wait... what?" David was the one to break the haunting silence.

"So, she wasn't a friend of Seb. She was his wife?" Aidan looked lost entirely. "Why? Why would she lie about that?"

The question was left lingering in the air for a moment before Gunvor finally collected herself.

"Maybe she suspected that her husband was into men and had a hard time accepting it like many others. Per's father almost threw me out of his office when I asked him if Per had ever been to a gay club. It's not pleasant having an unfaithful partner. For her, maybe the fact it was with men made it even worse."

"But that doesn't really explain anything. Why was she pretending to be his friend? To use me to look for him? Because she couldn't get herself to tell you guys at the agency that he was gay?"

"Something like that, probably. Maybe you were more kind and helpful than she'd anticipated anyone to be. She was out there alone, looking for someone that had let her down but whom she still cared for. And then she met you, a warm and helpful friend who gave her attention, company, and sound advice. Maybe she just couldn't resist that. And all of a sudden, you were both entangled in her lie."

Aidan suddenly looked more at ease.

"I suppose that makes sense. No wonder she has always seemed so mysterious."

"That's why she wouldn't tell you she lives in Fruängen." Hampus filled in.

"But they don't live in Fruängen. They live in a house in Bromma." Gunvor was sure. The agency always vetted their clients before they took on a case.

"Bromma? That's on the other side of town. What was she doing in Fruängen?"

There was a long silence before David said what they were all thinking.

"Was she following us?"

CHAPTER 61

ALL THE GOOD intentions of structure and neat timelines went out the window the second they realized that not only were Per and Seb the same person, but so were Eva and Marie. It was complete chaos on the boat, and everyone was talking over everyone else without really getting anywhere. Gunvor was as confused and frustrated as everyone else, and it took her a while to realize that it was down to her to get everyone to calm down and find some kind of order in the discussion.

"Okay, stop! People, please! We need to talk one at a time. Right now, it's crucial that we work together. All I can think about is that there's still a killer on the loose. What are your thoughts, Aidan?"

"I don't know. I'm thinking about Marie. Eva. There is definitely something strange about her. Well, obviously, she tricked me. But... I don't know. I'm just so confused. I really don't know."

"Elin?"

"Looking at the passenger manifest, it's evident that Eva-Marie went out to Nämdö when Per was still on the island.

But they don't seem to have met. Why? Isn't that strange? It's definitely strange. And also, she pretended to be someone else when she was looking for Per, which I guess isn't illegal but definitely very shady—even with your explanation, I have a hard time seeing how that would make sense." Elin threw her arms up. "I don't know. Maybe we should try calling Per?"

"Thomas?" Gunvor was eager to keep the pace up.

"When you met Eva-Marie, she was sad and desperate. She knew that her husband was cheating on her with other men. Despite that, she went out looking for him. She probably wanted nothing more than to get him back."

"She hated the clubs we went to and the people there." Aidan countered.

"And yet she kept going there, in the hope of finding him. I'm guessing that's because she loves him."

"Why would she follow us, though?" Hampus cut in.

"Maybe she thought you knew more than you had told her, which in a way is true. And she was desperate. You're not always rational when you're desperate."

This made the others stop and think for a moment. Thomas' reasoning sounded plausible, but there were still pieces missing.

"What I don't understand is what she was doing at Nämdö that weekend if they didn't see each other?"

"They probably did. Maybe they'd planned a weekend out there together, but they got into a big fight. If she confronted him with some of the things we now know, that might have been what prompted him to run off, rather than telling her about Vera right away." Slowly, things were falling into place for Gunvor.

"What about the murders then, where do they fit in?" David looked up from the notes.

"I don't know if they do. The optics of it is one thing. It does look very suspicious that Per knew all these people. But it could all be coincidental. Hate crimes?"

"Three random hate crimes around one person in two weeks?" David looked skeptical.

"As I said, the optics of it is one thing, but these crazy coincidences happen all the time. But okay, for the sake of argument, let's say it's not a coincidence. In that case, we have the drug lead. We've suspected Felix to be dealing drugs from the very beginning. Maybe he and Per had a little business together, Morgan and Alexander might have been in on it too, and something went wrong. What if Per killed them? No, wait, he has an alibi in Sundsvall. Okay, what if they went in over their heads and got in trouble with their supplier?"

"Oh, yes." David filled in." Like on TV. Maybe they lost the drugs or something and had a week to pay up before the mob started killing them one by one. And Per is next. Does he even know that the others are dead since he's been away?"

"Let's not jump to any conclusions, but I agree with Elin. We should call Per. He could be in danger. If not, it would still be good to talk to him. It could bring some clarity to this mess." Gunvor nodded towards Elin.

"I think you're right..." That was all Hampus got to say before Gunvor cut him off mid-sentence with a shrill voice.

"Shit! Vera!" Gunvor had suddenly realized, with horror, that Vera was on her way to Nämdö. "Per and Eva-Marie are going to Nämdö today, maybe they're already there, and Vera is supposed to take the next ferry out and meet them on the island. Can someone check the departures? I'm calling Per right now.

CHAPTER 62

WHEN THE LITTLE ferry slowed down to dock at Sand, Per and Eva-Marie stood ready at the prow. Per peeked at his phone to see if Vera had called or texted. To his dismay, he realized the phone was dead. Damn it. Why had he not thought of charging it on the boat? He had been giving Eva-Marie all his attention. Eager to get her forgiveness.

A young man pulled out the gangway and inspected their tickets as they got off the boat. When Per took Eva-Marie's hand in his, he realized how long it had been since they had been walking like this, hand in hand. He cringed when he thought of the way he had treated her, taking her for granted, never giving her that little extra that was needed to keep a relationship alive. She had been forced to put up with a lot. He knew that. He was beyond grateful that she had stuck by his side all these years. That she had coped. He had told her that countless times in the last twenty-four hours.

Eva-Marie let go of his hand for a moment to move her shoulder bag from one side to the other, and while doing so, it accidentally bumped into Per.

"Ouch, jeez. What are you carrying around in that bag?"

Per exaggerated his reaction a little, as a joke, in an attempt to lighten the mood. Even though Eva-Marie had been very understanding and listened to everything he had to tell her, she still seemed a little heavy at heart. Per understood that it must have been rough to learn about his daughter. Not only because they never had any children of their own. Vera was and would always be a reminder of his unfaithfulness.

She had not said one harsh word to him, just listened. But he could tell that she was struggling. Eva-Marie had always been a little closed off. But since he came back, she had been uncharacteristically quiet, even for her.

"Just girl-stuff, none of your business." She offered when he questioned her.

He was delighted to get a response to his banter.

"I suppose not. Girls and their bags."

He laughed and saw that she was also smiling a little. It warmed his heart. He was thankful that they had been able to find their way back to each other so quickly. Although he had brought Vera back from Sundsvall, he had not, at first, been convinced Eva-Marie would agree to meet her. He had even come up with a plan B—bringing Vera to see her grandparents so that her trip would not have been in vain, even if Eva-Marie had refused to meet her. He was sure that his parents would be overjoyed with the news of a grandchild, regardless of who the mother was.

The night before, when he had returned from Sundsvall, he had been greeted by an empty house. When he texted Eva-Marie, asking where she was, she replied that she was on her way home. Short and causal. As if he had never been gone. It had taken about half an hour for her to get back. By that time, it was already past eleven o'clock in the evening, and he had thought it was odd that she was out so late. She was usually home at night, was she not? Then he realized he had no idea whether this was unusual or not because he was rarely home in the evenings himself. He had just always assumed she stayed home.

She had seemed pleased to have him back home. Not overjoyed, but in her own way. She did not ask him any questions but listened to his story. And he never asked her where she had been. He realized that would probably be out of line, considering his own disappearance.

When he had taken off to Sundsvall, it had seemed like the most natural thing in the world, considering the circumstances. There had been an evolution in his life. He had been given a daughter. Everything else could wait. It was not until he came home to the empty house, feeling a little uneasy that Eva-Marie had gone off somewhere without telling him, that he started contemplating whether it would have been nice of him to have taken the time to explain things to her before he left. At least he could have picked up when she had called.

They walked along the gravel road together until they came upon the path that led up to their house. The sun had just set behind the horizon, and it was getting darker outside by the minute. It did not bother them. They both knew the way well enough to be able to walk it blindfolded. Per filled his lungs with a deep breath of the pine-scented air. Eva-Marie let go of his hand and took the lead down the narrow path. Per smiled to himself. For once, he felt genuinely happy. Soon, his daughter would arrive. He could not believe he had only just met her. She had his smile, his eyes. She had his frown when she was deep in thought. Soon, they would all be together, all three of them. He and his girls.

He slowed his pace. Eva-Marie noticed and turned around.

"What?"

"Listen… Is there something else we need to talk about? I understand if you're mad at me or have things you want to say or ask me about. I would just like to have cleared the air between us before Vera arrives."

He looked at Eva-Marie with warmth, but she avoided eye-contact.

"It's fine. You're back now."

She turned back towards the house and started walking.

"Eva, please."

"I'm freezing."

CHAPTER 63

ALL EYES WERE on Gunvor as she dialed the number.

"Straight to voicemail."

It was a superfluous comment. Everyone had already understood why Gunvor hung up the call so quickly.

"My guess is that they took the ferry that departed from Saltsjöbaden at 2:15 p.m., which arrived at Sand 3:50 p.m. The next ferry leaves at 5:55 p.m. and arrives at 7:45 p.m. That's probably the one Vera is taking." Elin said while reading from the SL's online timetables on her phone.

"It would probably be a good idea to call Vera's mother."

Thomas said what they were all thinking. Gunvor picked up her phone again and found Annika's number.

"Do you mind if I make this call in private?"

"Oh, of course," Thomas got up and led Gunvor into his bedroom and closed the door behind her.

She sat down on the soft bed and looked out at the sunset over Stockholm as she listened to the signals and waited for Annika to pick up.

"Please pick up, please pick up." She whispered to herself.

But there was no answer. She sent a short text asking Annika to call her as soon as possible.

When she came back to the other room with the bad news, Thomas made a suggestion.

"Let's take a trip out there."

"What do you mean? How would we get there? Do you think we could make it to Saltsjöbaden in time for the next ferry?"

"I don't know if you've noticed, but we're already on a boat. We need to go through the lock to get to the archipelago, and there are some speed restrictions. But if we leave now, we'll get there ahead of Vera. No problem."

"But what would we do there? Ask him if he's sold any drugs recently? He would hardly admit to that, and at this point, all we have are speculations." Elin felt confused.

"Let me worry about that. I don't mind if they get mad at me as long as I know everyone is safe. If I can talk to Per alone, I can talk to him about the possible threat to his security without being condemning. I'm sure he won't admit to anything, but hopefully, he is at least concerned about Vera's safety.

CHAPTER 64

PER HAD NOT BEEN BOTHERED by the biting, salty wind on the short walk from the ferry to the house. The closeness to nature was what had made him get the house in the first place. But now they were inside. He looked forward to lighting up the fire and enjoying a glass of wine or two. Since they had installed the AC that could be controlled remotely via an app on the phone, to make sure the house had the right temperature when they arrived, there was no real need to use the fireplace. But there was something therapeutic about looking into a live fire and listening to the crackling sound of burning wood.

"Will you get the fire going if I get us some wine? Red or white?"

It was as if Eva-Maria had read his thoughts. Or maybe they just always did it this way—he was not quite sure.

"Red. It goes with the weather. You can feel the winter coming."

Per picked up his phone and looked around for the charger.

"Give it to me. It's in the kitchen. I'll charge it for you."

Eva-Marie grabbed the phone from his hands and disappeared into the kitchen. Per wanted to protest. He had to stay close to the phone in case Vera called. But he did not want to risk getting into a conflict with Eva-Marie. Vera would not be there for another few hours anyway. He could let the phone charge in the kitchen for a bit and then get it.

He reached for a vinyl record and put it in place on the turntable. He lowered the volume before turning it on, remembering he had played at full blast the last time he was there. Soon Nina Simone´s deep voice filled the room.

I put a spell on you....

He took his time preparing the fireplace. It was a little ceremony that he had developed over the years that gave him satisfaction. When he was done, he lit a long match and watched as the flame quickly spread. He remained in front of the fireplace for a good while, watching the fire take hold of the larger pieces of wood, listening to the pops and crackles. When he realized Eva-Marie was taking a long time in the kitchen, he turned around to call for her but winced when he discovered that she was standing right behind him with two glasses of wine in her hands.

"Oh, I didn't hear you come in."

She smiled faintly and handed him one of the glasses. Then she wrapped herself in one of the white blankets that hung over the armrest on the sofa and got comfortable among the cushions.

"Cheers."

She raised her glass and took a sip. He followed suit.

"Cheers, darling."

He gave her a loving smile and took a deep gulp of the wine. He really preferred white wine. It was just that he associated it so much with the nightclubs. It felt better to stay away from it now that he was trying to transform himself into a family man. He took a few more sips, trying to ignore the coarse taste he knew he should appreciate. The important thing was that he got to relax a little. Getting tipsy was out of the question. Not now, when Vera was coming. He just wanted to calm the nerves a little. Vera was not a young child either, for that matter. Maybe she could try a small glass too. Surely it must be better for the youth to try a bit of alcohol at home to see what it does to you, rather than getting completely wasted on some contraband liquor with their irresponsible friends.

He realized his mind was wandering and looked up at Eva-Marie. She was watching him. He could not make out what mood she was in, a problem he often had with her. Sometimes she would seem angry but insist she was happy. Now, he thought, he could see the residue of a smile. She patted the seat next to her. He got up from the floor and sat down on the sofa with his glass reached held out. As she met it with hers, the glasses made a faint clinking sound. They had another sip. It occurred to Per that red wine seems to have a quicker effect than white wine for some reason. However, he could not quite palate that strange taste that lingered on the tongue.

Eva-Marie unwrapped herself from the blanket and reached for his glass. He watched as she walked out to the kitchen. Still well kept. Fit. He could not even remember the last time he had seen her naked. All that would change now, but it was best to take it slow. One step at a time. For both their sakes. It would be like rediscovering each other. No need to rush things like overly eager teenagers.

When she came back to the sofa, Per did his utmost to keep his attention on her. There was no need to talk. So much had already been said in the last twenty-four hours. At least on his part. It had been so liberating to tell her everything about his first meetings with Vera that he had not really noticed Eva-Marie's response. Had she even said anything? Nothing that had made an impression on Per anyway. He had just been relieved that she did not scold him. And that she had not left him. Maybe it was best to make sure everything really was alright, one last chance to clear the air before Vera arrived. Then they could close the door to the past and focus on the future.

"How are you feeling, sweetheart? Is there anything you want to talk about before our new family member arrives? Or anything you want to ask me?"

Eva-Marie just looked at him with her intense eyes. Suddenly her fingers wandered up to her neck, and she started fiddling with her necklace. It had been a habit of hers for as long as he could remember. It was not until he saw the little silver angel hanging from the chain that he realized something was wrong. Very, very wrong.

CHAPTER 65

THEY MADE it through the lock at Hammarby quicker than Gunvor had anticipated. However, it was not fast enough to get to Saltsjöbaden before the ferry to Nämdö departed. For a while, Thomas had been hopeful that they would be able to get there in time to board the ferry. That way, they would have been able to keep an eye on Vera discreetly. Instead, they would now have to try to get to the harbor in Sand before the ferry.

Elin had borrowed a dark green cardigan from Thomas and sat cooped up next to him in the wheelhouse. David was there too. He felt like he could never get tired of the view from the boat. His only previous experience had been a few rides with canoes and paddleboats on school excursions as a kid. He had always dreamed of having a boat like this.

As soon as he stepped aboard, he had been obsessed with the idea of going for a ride. He was more than delighted that the fantasy had become a reality so quickly. The fact that they were running against the clock only made it more exciting.

Thomas was not shy on the throttle. David assumed he

was driving well beyond the speed limit, but it did not bother him in the least. He enjoyed the boat's rocking motions and the lights from the city, and as they came further out, the occasional houses and lanterns reflected in the black water.

"This is Skurusunden."

Thomas gestured at the nautical chart before making a right turn in through a narrow inlet.

"Värmdöleden." He pointed at a large bridge ahead of them.

Suddenly the engine started coughing, and a few seconds later, it went quiet.

"Fuck!"

CHAPTER 66

PER HAD TROUBLE MOVING. His body felt heavy and sluggish. Eva-Marie had taken the glass from his hand. That was good of her. He would probably not have been able to hold on to it. The red wine would have made a terrible stain on the white sofa. However, he could really use another sip. That salty taste made him thirsty.

"Darling. The necklace?"

"Yes, what about my necklace?"

Eva-Marie's tone was stern and short. Not that it was anything unusual about that. They had been talking to each other like that for years. That was one of the things he wanted to change now. Was that so hard for her to see? Why did this woman always have to be so difficult?

"I thought you lost it."

For a second Per got nervous that he had been exposed. But no, that was impossible.

"Well, I found it again."

"Oh. That's good. Where was it? Under the bed?"

He thought she must have bought a new one. He clearly

remembered that she had asked him where he had gotten it. She must have purchased a new one but did not want to lose face by admitting to it.

For some reason, his thoughts started to feel heavy and sluggish too. How could he be this intoxicated from just a bit of wine? Sure, he had a beer on the ferry over but had never had any problems holding his liquor before.

"How could you? After all the shit I've done for you."

Eva-Marie's tone was more than stern now. There was an annoying, hysterical overtone in her voice.

"Everything you've done for me?" Per tried to laugh, but it came out as a croak. Why was his body disobeying him like this? And why was Eva-Marie trying to pick a fight today of all days? This was *his* day.

"You're the one that lives off me, not the other way around, Eva. And you're not even doing any chores because I'm paying someone else for that. So please, tell me about everything you've done for me."

"I make you look normal. Isn't that why you keep me around? To have someone to cover up for your deviant life. And now you want to drag an innocent girl into this mess?"

"It's my daughter. She's family."

"As if you've ever cared for anyone but yourself."

"But...."

"Are you going to make her sign a prenup too so that you won't have any responsibility for her either once you get tired of her?"

"Is this about money now? Have I not always given you whatever you've pointed at?"

"Yes, but nothing is ever really mine, is it? Not even this." She held up the necklace.

Per was still not sure whether she really knew, and he was

not about to incriminate himself by saying anything about it unless she presented some kind of evidence.

"Well, you're not the one busting your ass at the shipping company, are you?"

Eva-Marie scoffed and got up to leave the room.

CHAPTER 67

ELIN AND DAVID stared perplexedly at Thomas. His never-ending array of curse words was so out of character for him. Even though neither of the two knew anything about boating, it did not really take an experienced sailor to realize that the motor breaking down at sea was not great.

Thomas slammed his fists on the wheel as he continued swearing.

"Thomas," Elin got up and placed a hand on his shoulders. "I get that this is frustrating, but we need to focus and start looking for a solution. Do you have any idea what could be wrong with the engine?"

David was impressed with the way she handled the situation.

"I don't know. Shit." Thomas ran his fingers through his hair over and over....

" Okay, that's fine. Let's try googling it and see if we can find anything. What's the brand of the engine?"

"Bavaria."

"Okay. Bavaria. Great." Elin started typing on her phone.

"Let me know if you think of anything. Is there anyone we could call to ask about this? Do you have a service engineer or anything?"

Gunvor came up the stairs with an inquiring expression on her face, but David quickly ushered her back again.

"Come on, let's talk about it downstairs."

"Why have we stopped?"

"We have an engine failure, as you may have noticed. Thomas doesn't know why, so let's give them some space to figure it out.

"I'll help. I'm fairly good with machines." Aidan got up from the table without waiting for anyone's approval and disappeared up the stairs.

"I'm rather good at changing flat tires on my bike. Do you think it could be a flat tire? Should I join the rescue rangers up there?"

Gunvor giggled at Hampus' joke, but David was not amused. He would have loved to be a part of the so-called rescue rangers. All three of them were anxiously hoping the others knew what they were doing up there in the wheelhouse.

CHAPTER 68

"EVA-MARIE!" Per called out.

Eva-Marie was still in the kitchen. If he had the energy, he would have followed her out there. He just felt so tired if he could only rest for a little longer. When she finally returned to the living room, he decided to try and make peace with her. Her nagging and ungratefulness were frustrating, but he would not let that ruin his plans.

"My darling Eva-Marie. I know I haven't always been easy to live with. I know that you've put up with a lot. But you've always seemed alright with it. I hope I've given you at least a little bit of what you've been looking for." Per still felt light-headed, and his speech was slurred, but that did not matter. The important thing was for him to get his point across. To make her understand that he was serious. "You know it was my father who insisted on that prenup. Say what you will about him, but he is the one who built the fortune. Without him, there would not even be any money to fight over, right?"

He tried to give her a loving smile but had trouble fixating his eyes. She did not look very convinced.

"Your father has always pushed you around. You're as afraid of him now as you were when we met. Is it for his benefit you married me in the first place?"

"What? No." The conversation was not going in the direction Per had planned at all.

"It is because you want him to think that you're normal. Is this all about him?"

"Honey, what? No, that's not it at all. What do you mean, normal? I just want us to become a real family. You, me, and Vera. Can't you see she's the last missing piece of the puzzle?"

"She is not a piece of any puzzle. She's your receipt for having cheated on me."

"She's a kid! Our kid."

"Right." Eva-Marie stood up and disappeared into the kitchen once again. Per attempted to follow, but he could not get up on his feet. Soon. He would go after her soon and make everything okay. He just needed to rest, just for a minute.

CHAPTER 69

THOMAS CAME FLYING DOWN the stairs and into the bedroom. Gunvor did not want to hold him up by asking questions, but his great ardor made her feel hopeful that they were nearing a solution to the engine problem. There was a loud bang when he slammed open a wooden chest so that the heavy lid crashed into the wall behind. Thomas pulled one unidentifiable object after another out of the chest and threw them all on the floor and his bed in a frenzy. At last, he seemed to have found what he was searching for.

"I had a spare!" He shouted out. This was met with cheers from the wheelhouse upstairs. Gunvor, David, and Hampus witnessed the whole scene without making a sound. It seemed more important that they got the boat up and running again than knowing all the details of what was going on.

"New spark plug." Thomas said with a grin as he passed them on his way back to the wheelhouse. "Should have gotten them replaced a long time ago."

The three of them sat in silence and listened to the others working upstairs. Thomas felt like an idiot for having blanked when the engine stopped and assured the others that he really knew more about mechanics than it seemed. He had just panicked at the thought of not getting them to Nämdö in time. Aidan and Elin did their best to cheer him up, and it hit Gunvor how lucky she was, after all. She had been a lone wolf for so many years, and now, somehow, she was surrounded by all these lovely, good-hearted people.

When the engine suddenly came to life with a roar, they all let out a sigh of relief. But this was not the time to celebrate. Not just yet. She closed the door behind her in the bedroom and dialed Manuel's number.

CHAPTER 70

PER WOKE UP WITH A START. He must have dozed off. After another failed attempt at getting off of the couch, he looked at his wristwatch. It was probably time to go and meet Vera by the ferry soon. But for some reason, the watch did not make sense. His mind felt like goo.

"Eva-Marie?"

When she appeared in the doorway, he sensed that something terrible had happened, but he could not remember it.

"The news is on."

She sat down next to him and scrolled through the channels on the little TV set next to the fireplace.

A man's body has been found on a sailing boat, anchored in the middle of the fairways along Saltsjöbaden. Preliminary forensic investigations show that the death occurred about two weeks ago. Around the same time the boat appeared, according to local residents. The victim has been identified as Felix Wiik. Police are asking the public to come forward with any information....

Per had trouble following the segment. The voice was

talking so quickly. And that boat. There was something familiar about it. He just could not place it. It was when Felix's face appeared on the screen that chills ran up his spine.

"What the... Eva?"

Eva-Marie was not looking. She had started digging through her shoulder bag for something.

"Ah, here it is."

She held up the blood-stained ax in front of Per.

"Okay then, Honey. I'm off to see Vera. Don't you worry. I'll bring her back in one piece. Or more." She smiled triumphantly.

"Please. Not Vera. She's the dearest thing I've got."

A light went out in Eva-Marie's eyes.

"No, the dearest thing you had, you ruined a long time ago. You've exhausted your rights to have anything more."

CHAPTER 71

WHEN THEY APPROACHED NÄMDÖ, everyone was up in the wheelhouse with Thomas. Because of the engine failure, they could not catch up with the ferry, but they could see it in the distance now.

Gunvor had spoken to Manuel. Despite her best efforts, she had not been able to convince him that there was any imminent danger. At long last, he had agreed to call one of his buddies at the coast guard, who had made the same assessment, but told them that they had a patrol nearby that they could call in, should the situation get out of hand.

She did not know what more they could do. All they had were theories and speculations. She hesitated to call Vera. If Manuel was right and everything was alright at the house, she would undoubtedly stir up quite a mess by asking Vera to stay on the ferry and send her off, alone, further out the archipelago. It would take hours to get her back.

"There it is. Sand." Thomas pointed to a landing stage further up the shoreline with someone waiting on the ferry.

Gunvor squinted, but it was too far away to make out if it could be Per.

CHAPTER 72

THE FERRY WAS TEDIOUS. The trip felt so much longer now that she was alone, and it was dark outside. The last time she had taken the trip, it had been a beautiful day, and she had been accompanied by Per. Dad. She tried entertaining herself on the phone but kept going back to counting the minutes to the arrival at Sand.

Calling him dad felt so natural. Even though she had had another dad her whole life. It was not like Per was going to replace him—it was just that now she had two dads. She could see herself in Per. All that restlessness, her longing for adventure, and the carefreeness her family was always nagging her about. It all made sense now. Per had experienced so much, and he had expensive things and knew about all the cool clothes. Before he had driven her back to Sundsvall, he had shown her all the good stores in Stockholm and gotten her exclusive clothes from brands she had only seen on celebrities. Nothing like what she was used to at home.

She felt terrible for taking off to Stockholm without saying anything to her mom. She was well aware that Annika had been worried sick. But she had wanted to do it in her own way, without interference, and she was glad to have done it. The results had been better than she had ever even hoped.

Once her mom had calmed down, they all had a great time together in Sundsvall. Even her dad, her other dad, Ove, had been on his best behavior, and despite all their differences, he and Per had seemed to enjoy each other's company. Everything had been perfect. It was not until these last couple of hours she had started to feel a little funny. She could not quite get her head around why it was so important that she took the ferry alone, rather than just going with Per and his wife. And why had he not called? He promised that he would call. What if they changed their minds and had not even gone to Nämdö? Then she would be all alone on that island. Per had shown her where they hid a spare key, but she was not even sure she would find her way to the house in the darkness.

She rechecked her phone. Not that she would have ever missed a text or call, she had the volume set to max. Still nothing. The ferry would be arriving at Nämdö any minute now. She had to call him, and if he did not pick up, she would have to call her mom for help.

When the phone suddenly started ringing in her hands, she was so startled that she almost dropped it.

CHAPTER 73

THE HATRED HAD CONSUMED EVA-MARIE. The disappointment, sadness, the feeling of inadequacy, and betrayal that had loomed over her for most of her life were all gone. There was no plan, just scattered thoughts. Pictures of violence in her head that would not go away. All she had wanted to do was to find Per and bring him back and save the marriage.

Per had fallen asleep again. She left him on the sofa. Even if he woke up, he would not be able to move. It had proven harder than she thought, controlling someone with drugs. Especially since she did not have any first-hand experience. On the other hand, she had been surprised by how easy it had been to get access to the drugs. She must have seemed like an unlikely customer. For a while she was worried that they had tricked her and given her something else. It was not until Per began slurring his speech that she felt assured that it was actually GHB she had put in his wine.

Eva-Marie had almost reached the landing platform when she checked her wristwatch. The girl would arrive any minute now. It was a cold night, and a biting breeze blew in from the sea. A person would not survive for long in these waters. Freezing to death was apparently a pretty decent way to go. So was drowning.

The lanterns of the ferry were now clearly visible as it approached the island. Game time.

CHAPTER 74

THE NEXT TIME Per woke up, he had no idea where he was. The room felt vaguely familiar somehow. But it was almost impossible to get any two thoughts to line up. It was not until a few minutes later he finally realized where he was. The summer house. But what was he doing in the summer house all by himself?

Suddenly the memories came creeping back, and along with it, the panic.

"Eva-Marie?"

No answer. Not a sound. Had she left the house?

The ax. Why had she taken the ax? His attempts to get up were futile, but he managed to muster enough energy to slide down on the floor after a while. Slowly, slowly he crawled towards the drawer. The whole house was spinning, and it made him want to throw up. He closed his eyes but continued his slow crawl. With one last effort, he stretched up his arm and managed to get the landline phone. Somehow, he still remembered the number.

"Dad?"

"Honey... Don't get off the boat. Eva-Marie... Eva-Marie... she's gone mad."

The next second, everything faded into darkness again.

CHAPTER 75

EVA-MARIE RECOGNIZED the young man who operated the gangway. He often worked on this route. The Johansson's, who lived up the road, and greeted her politely as they passed by, were the only ones to get off the ferry.

"Hello, are you boarding or what?"

The young man waved at her.

She did not understand. Had Vera forgotten to get off the boat? Or was she getting off at Solvik instead? Either way, she could not just stand there looking like an idiot. So, she made up her mind.

"Oh, yes. Sorry."

She boarded the ferry just as it was ready to take off. Eva-Marie looked around the café as she was purchasing her ticket. There were only a few passengers, and none of them a teenage girl.

She put the ticket in her wallet to avoid it getting wrinkled, just as usual. Once she had secured the wallet in the bag, she left the café to systematically search the ferry.

CHAPTER 76

FROM HER SPOT on the now completely dark sundeck, Vera had a good view of the ferry stop as they approached land. She was not sure what Eva-Marie looked like, but only one person was waiting at the stop. A middle-aged woman. The panic, which already had her in a firm grip, grew. Just a few more minutes, then she would be safe, and she could call her mom and the police to make sure dad was safe. Eva-Marie would never see her up there on the dark deck.

The ferry docked, and only two people got off the ferry. Every second felt like an eternity. Why were they not taking off? What were they waiting for?

Suddenly, Eva-Marie started walking up the gangway.

"Shit, shit, shit." Vera looked desperately around her. There was nowhere to hide.

CHAPTER 77

THEY DECIDED THAT GUNVOR, Aidan, Elin, and David would run to the house. Thomas and Hampus stayed on the boat and kept the engine running in case they would have to make a speedy exit. Best to be prepared for anything.

She managed to keep a good pace through the grove despite the pain that pierced Gunvor's knee like arrowheads. The lights in the house were on, but they could not see anyone inside through the windows. Gunvor knocked on the door. Silence. She pushed the handle gently. Unlocked. The four of them tiptoed into the house.

There was an eerie silence. Gunvor started thinking that maybe this was all a big mistake. Of course, Per and Eva-Marie were just down at the ferry stop, greeting Vera. Suddenly there was a moan coming from the living room. As Gunvor approached the room, there was Per on the floor. No blood or visible injuries.

"Quickly, search the house for the other two!"

Gunvor gave the order as she kneeled beside Per.

"Per? Per! Can you hear me?"

At first, he just groaned. But as she shook him lightly, he seemed to come around, looking at Gunvor with hazy eyes.

"Per! Why are you on the floor? Where is Vera?"

"The ferry... I told her to stay on the ferry...."

"Why? Where is Eva-Marie?"

Per closed his eyes again. Gunvor slapped him on the cheek in an attempt to wake him up, at which he stared at her with horror.

"Stop her! You've got to stop her. She has an ax."

"Shit!" Gunvor got up. "Guys, we need to get to Solvik! NOW!"

She left Per on the floor and ran for the door. Aidan came stumbling down the stairs.

"What happened?"

Gunvor was already out on the lawn.

"David! Elin!"

David and Elin came running from the backside of the house.

"It's Eva-Marie. She's going to hurt Vera. They're on the ferry. You need to run and catch the ferry at Solvik. I can't run that far. I'll meet you there with Thomas and the boat as soon as we can get there. Just follow the road and take a right at the church. Go!"

CHAPTER 78

WHEN THOMAS and Hampus saw Gunvor come running down the slope towards the boat, they realized that something must have happened, and Hampus jumped onto land and started running to meet up with her.

"No, we've got to go!" She gestured to him to turn around. "We need to catch up with the ferry. Vera and Eva-Marie…" She was not able to finish the sentence. She tried to catch her breath as Hampus helped her aboard the boat, and as soon as they had gotten into the wheelhouse, Thomas had the engine in full throttle.

CHAPTER 79

EVA-MARIE HAD RANSACKED the whole ferry. No sign of the girl. She headed to the restrooms, the only place she had not searched. There were three bathrooms in a row in a small hallway. Two of the stalls were occupied. Eva-Marie positioned herself at the end of the hallway, pretending to wait for her turn in case someone who was not Vera would go in or out. After a couple of minutes, an elderly lady came out of one of the stalls. Eva-Marie waited patiently for her to leave before she knocked discreetly on the remaining stall door.

"Vera?"

When there was no answer, she knocked again, harder, with a stern tone in her voice.

"Vera. Come on out here."

The ferry rocked. Eva-Marie peeked out from the hallway to see what was going on. They must be approaching the next stop. Most of the passengers on the nearly empty ferry seemed to be gathering their coats and belongings to get off the boat.

Eva-Marie reached for the ax in her bag.

"Vera. I've got a pretty big ax here. If you're not opening

that door right now, I will chop right through it, and believe me, you don't want me to start chopping. Do you understand? Now get out here, you little shit."

The rage had caught up to Eva-Marie again. She banged on the door so that the whole construction started rattling. There was a quiet click when the door unlatched from the inside. Eva-Marie took a step back. Just to be safe. She did not know Vera—she could come charging out of the stall with a knife for all she knew. But she did not. The door opened very slowly, and she saw a pair of big, frightened eyes looking at her. They belonged to a face that looked like a carbon copy of Per as a young teenager. Eva-Marie was so taken aback by this that she completely lost her train of thought. To think that a young girl could look so much like Per. A young Per. The face she had fallen so madly in love with all those years ago. The fragile innocence. The small-boned lineaments. The things that had withered away from Per's own face over the years now, making it bloated and dull, ruined by late nights and alcohol.

"Marie."

She did not hear them come up behind her all of a sudden. They just stood there, Aidan and those two youths they had run into at Side Track. The ones Aidan had pretended not to know. Another betrayal, of course. She grabbed the ax with both hands, letting the bag fall to the floor.

"Marie. Can you please put down the ax?"

Aidan's voice was demanding. Eva-Marie suddenly felt so very tired. The ferry rocked again as they took off to sea.

"Marie."

As he took a step closer, reaching for the ax, she raised it over her head.

"Get off me!"

"Marie, don't make this worse." Aidan tried to keep a

steady voice. Even though his entire being was trembling in panic. He glanced at Vera. She looked unharmed, horrified, but unharmed.

"You were supposed to be my friend." Eva-Marie looked accusingly at Aidan.

"I am, I still am. I want to help you."

When he took another step towards her, she reacted in a split second by swinging the ax at him. He did his best to throw himself out of reach from the blade as it came towards him at blazing speed, but it caught him on the outer edge of his shoulder and ran down along his arm. He fell to the floor with a howl. When Eva-Marie raised the ax again, David and Elin grabbed Aidan in a hurry and dragged him out of reach, as Vera shut the door to her stall again.

A new wave of rage and hate gave Eva-Marie renewed strength. They would not stop her now, not after all they had done to her. She slammed the ax into the stall door with a force that sent splinters flying through the air. Vera was screaming. She had to shut her up once and for all.

The boat rocked heavily once again. Now what? She paused and peeked out to the café and the entrance of the boat. Aidan's young friend had managed to drag him halfway into the café, leaving a thick trail of blood. Everyone stared at her. Silent. Scared.

She shrugged and got back to finish her work. She raised the ax above her head once again and charged with all her power. Somehow the ax got stuck in the stall door. She yanked and pulled, but it would not come out. She let the ax go and started banging on the door with her bare knuckles until they were a bloody mess.

"Come out here, you little bastard!" She was screaming now. But it was as if her energy was starting to drain.

The ferry kept rocking. Looking at the entrance again, she could see another boat side by side with the ferry. Someone was entering the boat. She went back into the hallway, but she was distracted. What was happening out there? When she heard someone approaching, she turned around and immediately recognized Gunvor.

"Is everyone against me? Why isn't anyone going after Per? Don't you get that this is all his fault?"

But Eva-Marie could see in their eyes that Gunvor did not get it. None of them did. She suddenly rushed past Gunvor and took off up the stairs and out onto the sundeck.

CHAPTER 80

GUNVOR RAN AFTER EVA-MARIE, but she was nowhere to be seen. Hampus, who had followed right behind her, crouched down to check under the rows of benches. There was nowhere to hide. Nowhere to go, except over the rails, down in the water.

Thomas drove slowly around in circles. When the situation was thoroughly explained to the captain of the little ferry, he turned on the searchlights and let them sweep across the sea's dark surface. Nothing. Eva-Marie had vanished.

When the coast guard eventually arrived, the group was escorted back to the Cedergrens' house. Per had regained consciousness, but the Coastguard thought it best to air shuttle him back to the city for a thorough examination. The same was true for Aidan. A crew member had managed to slow down the bleeding, but the blood loss had made him weak, and he needed stitches.

It had taken some convincing to get Vera to open up the door to the bathroom stall. However, once she realized the danger was over, she had calmed down pretty quickly. After a call with her mother, Annika, whom they finally managed to get a hold of, it was decided that Gunvor would take custody of Vera for the night. Annika would take the early morning train down to Stockholm to be there when the police questioned Vera.

It was well past midnight before they had all given their initial statements to the officers and were allowed to sail back to Stockholm. The whole gang was keeping Thomas company in the wheelhouse. Gunvor opened the boxed wine and handed out glasses. For Thomas and Vera, she had prepared a thermos of coffee in the little kitchenette. It had already been a long night, and there would be hours still before they got home.

"I can't believe it was her all along."

Gunvor said what everyone was thinking. Eva-Marie had killed three people in cold blood. Precisely what her plans had been for Vera, they would probably never know.

David shuddered at the thought of the look in Eva-Marie's eyes as she had swung the ax at Aidan.

"You can't help but wonder what pushed her over the edge."

"Maybe she really believed in her story about him just being depressed in the beginning. But by the time she met Aidan, she must have known. Perhaps it was too much for her to see the faces of the people Per had been sleeping around with." Gunvor speculated.

"But what about when she followed us to Fruängen? Do you think she would have attacked us?"

"Hampus told her that Per was too old for him. Maybe she was somehow offended that he didn't even want Per. Don't you remember the face she made when he said it?" Elin had noted Eva-Marie's reaction but had not realized the full meaning of it until now.

"So, what about Felix?"

"He was a sex worker, not a drug dealer. Per told me that before the helicopter arrived. He'd seen it all in the news too. How Eva-Marie found out about them, I don't know."

EPILOGUE
SATURDAY, OCTOBER 24

SHE HAS BEEN THINKING about it for a long time—about Per and his needs. Needs to which she has never responded. She has come to the conclusion that she is partially responsible for his behavior. In a way, she has forced him to look elsewhere for someone to quench his thirst. For a long time she did not even care. She thought it was fine, let him have sex with others if that kept the pressure off her. It only proves what a man he is.

Eva-Marie is nothing like Per. Never has been. The truth is, she is the peculiar one. She loves Per, but she cannot stand intimacy. Never could. Not with anyone. Not that there have been that many, but still, enough to figure out that the problem lies within her.

Lately, she has been worried. He seems to have become more and more absent. Is he dreaming of a woman that can fulfill his every need? He has already passed fifty. He's not a youth anymore. Sure, he is still fit and attractive and charming. But all those late nights must be taxing, even for him.

The pursuit is probably exciting in itself. But it must get

exhausting year after year. She has always been hopeful that his lust would fade away with age. It seems like it's a wish that will remain unfulfilled.

So, it is time. Time for her to give him what he wants. Bite the bullet and do what she needs to do to keep her husband and make him happy. And her life? She needs this too so she can keep the life she has. The prenuptial agreement he made her sign when they got married would leave her with next to nothing.

He does not know that she is coming. He has made it clear that he wishes to be alone in the cabin buried in work. Her guess is that he wants to be by himself, away from her. They are at a crossroads. If she does not manage to bring him back in now, she never will.

The other passengers on the ferry are probably wondering why the woman in Wellingtons and a well-worn parka is made up so nicely. They do not know about the newly acquired underwear. The only thing she is wearing beneath her coat is lace and other rubbish. With the down parka buttoned up to her neck, she gazes out at the sunset while her thoughts are frequently disturbed by the stiff bra chafing against her breasts.

The ferry ride turns into torment. The excitement of getting to the cabin and showing off her surprise is mixed with equal parts anxiety. As always, when she is worried, her hand finds its way to her neck. But the necklace is missing, the necklace Per gave her, the one with the little silver angel that always brings her comfort when she is nervous or down.

What if he does not like the surprise? What if he is not attracted to her anymore? The thought makes her nauseous. No, he is still with her. Despite all the other women, he is still with her.

The ferry finally docks. She is the only person to get off at

Sand—there is light coming from the windows of the little red cabin next to the landing. More often than not, the neighbors will peek out to see who is arriving and greet them with a friendly gesture. Not tonight.

She follows the familiar dirt road, then the narrow path through the forest leading up to their house. Her forest. The scent of pine and moss calms her nerves. She takes a deep breath, and a faint smile finds its way to her lips.

Lights. The lights are on in the house. They do not have any close neighbors, so they never bother to close the curtains or the blinds. She stops outside one of the windows and looks for him. She imagines him sitting on the couch with the laptop on his knee, lost in his work. A glass of wine on the table. Maybe a small bowl of olives.

Then she sees him. His torso. It is nothing like what she had just imagined. He is naked. When she finally manages to focus her eyes, she realizes that his body is in motion. Slow pulses coming from the hips. Suddenly he jerks his head back and lifts his right arm, putting the hand on his neck. It looks stupid.

Another person that has been out of her vision until now but apparently has been sitting in front of Per gets up from the floor. They kiss.

What the hell?

Her whole body stops. She is unable to move. Unable to breathe. An iron fist around her throat. Her eyes cannot let go of the two men in the living room. They are doing things she had never even been able to imagine men doing to each other.

At that moment, she is losing everything. Torn apart by sorrow, disgust, betrayal, and anger. Ruined. Standing there in the ridiculous set of underwear that she hates, but she got them anyway—for him.

She stays rooted to her spot; it does not go on for much longer. They get dressed. She is frozen to the ground in the grove. The men are talking and laughing inside the cabin. Per hands over what looks like an envelope. The other man takes a quick look at the contents and nods. A settlement has been made. Both parties seem happy.

They disappear out of her line of sight. After a few minutes, she hears the front door open. Even though it is dark by now, and she is invisible in the grove, she takes cover behind a big pine tree.

"Thank you, Felix."

"Yeah, thanks."

She hears the men laugh and say their goodbyes before the door finally slams shut. The man starts making his way down to their jetty, the man who has just done the unthinkable. She follows him as silently as she can. As she passes the woodshed, she almost subconsciously pulls the ax from the woodblock.

He has already started the boat's engine when she descends from the shadows. He stares at her in surprise as she jumps aboard.

"Help." She whispers in feigned terror and points towards land.

He immediately turns around, his eyes searching the darkness. That is all she needs to make her final decision. She strikes him as hard as she can. He is on the floor with the first blow, but she cannot stop. Not until he lies perfectly still. Not until he has drawn his last breath.

When she is done, she navigates the boat out of the bay with a deft hand. The darkness is all around her. Not a living soul in sight. She has not been out on the sea for a long time, but she still has the knack. The knack for sailing. The knack for being alone. Abandoned. Invisible. Her breathing is forced. Her chest is heavy; she has to struggle to find air.

The boat's cockpit is messy. Colorful flyers are lying around higgledy-piggledy. She tries to sort them in neat stacks on the table. Calm down. It takes a minute before she realizes what the flyers are. They are advertising meeting places for men. She swipes them all down into the sludge on the floor, most of them anyway, a few of them she puts in her coat pocket.

She is thankful that no one seems to notice her as she jumps ashore at Båtmans Backe, arriving back shortly after midnight. She is thankful that the man had a long raincoat stashed in the boat so she can cover up the stains as she gets on the first train at Neglige back to the city. And that is the only thing for which she is thankful.

AFTERWORD

Another case is closed. This one will probably stay in the thoughts of Gunvor Ström and her team for a while. Make them search for answers they will never get. But life will go on, and they will slowly forget.

Gunvor follows Kjell back to the Canary Islands again and stays longer than she ever has before. She is enjoying vacationing in her paradise but at the same time longs to be of use.

Elin travels to the Canary Islands with her school mates. David and Aidan also make a quick decision to reunite with their friends and have a few days off.

They all expect lazy days in the sun, enjoying each other's company.

They could not be more wrong

ACKNOWLEDGMENTS

My special thanks to:

My publisher—Publish Authority—because they share their great knowledge and are my wise guides through the winding paths in the land of marketing.

Ylva Rosén for her sharp eye in the proofreading.

Nancy Lanning, Publish Authority Editor, for her professional editing work and invaluable suggestions for improvements.

ABOUT THE AUTHOR

Swedish author Luna Miller (pseudonym) specializes in Nordic Noir and is the writer of the international best-seller *Three Days in September,* and is one of the authors of the international anthology *Love Unboxed 2. Looking for Alice,* the first book in the series of the private detective Gunvor Ström, was published in March 2020.

In mid-life, after experiencing life and adventure throughout Europe, India, China, Pakistan, Iran, Thailand and a host of other countries, with her studies, children and work, Luna found quality time to write her debut novel *Three Days in September,* followed by *Den som ger sig in I leken,* – the original Swedish precursor of *Looking for Alice.*

Because You're Mine is Miller's second book in the Gunvor Ström series, and. her next book is to be released in early 2022.

For more, please visit LunaMiller.com

THANK YOU FOR READING

Publish Authority
If you enjoyed *Because You're Mine*, we invite you to share your thoughts and reactions online and with family and friends.

CPSIA information can be obtained
at www.ICGtesting.com
Printed in the USA
BVHW040917130321
602408BV00013B/724